MW01007835

MURDER ON THE BRANDYWINE

An Emily Menotti Mystery

by

MARYELLEN WINKLER

Also by Maryellen Winkler:

The Disappearance of Darcie Malone

What Killed Rosie?

Cruising to Death

Murder on the Brandywine
Copyright 2018, Maryellen Winkler
All rights reserved.

ISBN
978-1-935751-48-9 (paperback)
978-1-935751-49-6 (eBook)

Published by
Scribbulations LLC
Kennett Square, Pennsylvania
U.S.A.

This story is dedicated to my brother,
Henry, who wanted me to write a mystery
about a murder that takes places at Hagley Museum.
I tried, but Alicia insisted that
her story be told this way.

Acknowledgments

I would like to thank my friend, Donna Moe,
who once again agreed to be my First Look editor,
and Grace Spampinato, my editor,
who offered invaluable support and advice.

I lift my eyes to the stars
And long for my other home
Where I am known
Where I am cherished.

-mew

THE BRANDYWINE

The Brandywine River has always been a companion to my life. I was born in the Delaware Hospital, since rechristened the Wilmington Hospital, whose titian walls overlook the banks of the Brandywine River where it flows under the Washington Street Bridge. If you're standing on the bridge or below it, the hospital walls shoot up rampart-like above the river and its environs, sheltering a small graveyard where memories of battles lost and souls forsaken are buried. As if to mock the somberness of the scene, the river here gurgles and giggles around rough boulders and smooth pebbles, full of the vitality that the hospital patients nearby are fighting desperately to preserve.

I grew up within walking distance of the Brandywine. On a warm Sunday afternoon, while my mother napped, my father would walk my sister and me beneath the yellow-green leaves of the oak trees that lined both sides of Baynard Boulevard to the entrance to Brandywine Park at Eighteenth Street. We'd brush past the bushes and trees that lined the narrow cement path down the hill to North Park Drive. Then we'd pick our way through the bushes that clung to the riverbanks and play on the larger stones on the shore. In the spring, we watched kayak races. I was enthralled by the sunburnt men in bright jackets frantically propelling their narrow craft through the foaming rapids and guiding them under the Market Street bridge and into the calmer waters of the lower Brandywine where it meets up with the sluggish expanse of the Christina River.

In summer, we visited the Brandywine Zoo, and I gazed with a child's awe at the brown bear in his damp cave, or the tiger pacing back and forth in his iron-gated pen. Afterward, we might sit on the marble ledge of the fountain in Josephine Gardens and enjoy the cool spray.

In winter there were sled rides down Monkey Hill, as we held our breath against the icy wind and tugged on the crossbeams of our Flexible Flyers to avoid crashing into the trees at the bottom or the brick walls of the Monkey House, hence the name of the hill.

As a teenager, I crossed the Brandywine River twice a day as I trod Van Buren Street to and from Ursuline Academy. As an adult, I returned in September for the Brandywine Arts Festival.

I've taken the tours at Hagley Museum and Winterthur and attended the Wilmington Flower Market at nearby Rockford Park. Outside of the city, a favorite car ride is to follow Route 100 north out of Wilmington where it parallels the river through Montchanin; Chadds Ford; and up to Lenape, Pennsylvania.

To an outsider, it's a very ordinary, albeit, lovely river. Those interested in such things can Google its length and width, but I'm drawn not only to its beauty but also to its history. In 1777, General George Washington lost to the British at the Battle of Brandywine Creek. There are walking and driving tours throughout the Brandywine Valley if you want to immerse yourself in the history of the area. You can visit Brandywine Battlefield Park on Route 1 in Chadds Ford. Or visit nearby Valley Forge where the colonial troops nearly perished during that wretchedly frigid winter.

In 1802, the duPonts built their powder mills along the river and later established elaborate homes and gardens. Among the contributory waters to the Brandywine in Chester County, Pennsylvania, a visitor can find one of the duPonts most delightful and enduring legacies, Longwood Gardens.

To see the river best, you should board a canoe or inner tube from a point below the Brandywine River Museum in Chadds Ford and let the river carry you down to Delaware. On a scorching summer day, you can float beneath burgeoning black willows that shelter you from the sun, dip your hand into the Brandywine's cool green depths, or brave its rocky floor to walk and swim.

Stop for a picnic at Beaver Valley; then continue as the river broadens and deepens to where you'll disembark at Thompson's Bridge, just north of Brandywine Creek State Park. Allow plenty of time, as this trip could take several hours. Along the way, you may see the ghosts of Revolutionary War soldiers searching for their regiment, long-dead gunpowder workers seeking their families, or a twenty-something girl with blonde hair who thought she would live forever.

Maryellen Winkler

Saturday Night

Alicia stood in front of the bathroom mirror and thought about opposites: what was beautiful and what was not. She studied herself—turning left, then right. She did a pirouette, and as she turned she brought her hands up in the air, then gracefully let them fall at her sides as she came out of the turn. She then addressed her image—an image that always seemed to her attractive but was never attractive enough to win the admiration of the general male population. Yes, there had been boyfriends—an odd collection of dwarfs and carnival fodder with sweaty hands and open mouths. There was even a fiancé, and she loved him, but he lacked something she couldn't define.

She picked up the eyeliner pencil and slowly applied a thin line of Midnight Blue to each eyelid. She thought of another opposite, good and evil. She tried to be good. She'd always tried to please her father, her brother, her teachers, her employers. It was so exhausting to be good. And the world was so evil. Money, money, money. It was all sex and money. Sometimes she hated the world.

Alicia applied the Chestnut Brown mascara. She used brown because black created too stark a contrast with her blonde hair, hanging loose below her shoulders. Hair was another problem. She tried to curl it, tried to straighten it, but it always wound up in unruly waves. It was hopeless. Even when she was told she was beautiful, she knew she wasn't, certainly not like Reese Witherspoon or Jessica Alba.

She was excited about her plans for tonight, though. She was going to Brandywine Creek State Park to witness something she'd never seen before. Something mystical, magical, perhaps even life transforming. Maybe it would herald a new beginning.

She needed a new beginning. She'd made so many mistakes.

Slept with so many men—for all the wrong reasons. Like the song, she'd looked for love in all the wrong places. She'd been part of the problem, not the solution. A cliché. Her whole life had been a cliché. She sighed, and her sigh echoed around the world and down the ages to all the young women who had ever lived and died, disappointed in love, disappointed in themselves.

Alicia pulled up her top and turned around to view the new tattoo on her lower back. She touched one corner of it carefully. This was her banner of change. Her statement. She was going to be part of the solution now.

The needle had hurt, but it was a good hurt, a pleasurable hurt, the kind most people didn't understand. Like when she used to cut herself, which she hadn't done for years. But that one moment of pain was such a release, such a joy. In that nanosecond every other pain, doubt, and insecurity in her whole life receded and raised her to a climax of just one pain. Yes, it hurt, but it was real, not a lie, not a put on, not someone else's truth. It was her truth. And somehow, in her twisted universe of opposites, this pain was a victory and a consolation.

She heard the car horn honk outside. Her ride. She pulled down her top, grabbed her purse, and ran out the door.

CHAPTER ONE

THE BOY

Emily brought her Civic to a stop in the gravel parking lot of Brandywine Creek State Park. The morning sky was a clear azure blue, glittering with energy and possibilities. The sun, a golden orb, just barely brushed the treetops.

Emily spoke excitedly to her friend, Melinda, as they exited the car. "You won't believe Desmond's latest. Now I'm not allowed to use the washing machine." She twisted strands of light brown hair around her fingers as they crossed the parking lot, their steps resounding from squashed tiny daggers of sticks and stones.

"Tell me how you know this man again?" Melinda asked.

"We dated in high school, very hot and heavy, until he was sent to military school after he and his friends torched the sports equipment shack. It was either military or reform school. Desmond's parents could afford military."

"And how did you hook up with him again?"

They were approaching the trampled grass path to the Hawk Watch and upper meadow, Melinda lagging behind.

Emily turned around, walking backward, as she talked to Melinda. "When I was first transferred here from New Hampshire, I was looking for a room to rent and answered an ad in the *Wilmington Reporter*. You can't imagine how shocked we each were when I knocked and he opened the door. He's divorced now too, and his home is perfect: hardwood floors, screened-in back porch, a family room with a fireplace. My bedroom is small, but I'm usually just in there to sleep."

"Speaking of, have you slept with him yet?" The tone of her voice was jesting, but Emily sensed concern.

"No, I have not, but I'm considering it."

Melinda came to a stop just a few steps into the brown grass.

The sun caught her copper hair and gave off sparks. Her laugh lines morphed into a frown as she spoke. "There's so many people here, Emily. So many young men. They're wearing Revolutionary War uniforms, but all torn and dirty; then there are other men, in drab work clothes and dark aprons. They're shuffling about like they're lost."

Emily looked around at the empty park. It was nine o'clock in the morning. "I don't see anyone. Where are they?"

"They're not corporal. They're spirits, spirits of young men. Tell me about this park. What happened here?"

Emily was reminded that Melinda was not from Delaware. She was also a clairsentient and a physical medium. She was obviously seeing scenes from the past.

"We're a few miles downstream from the Battle of the Brandywine. You may be seeing soldiers who died in the Revolutionary War. You could also be seeing workmen from the mills. After the war, in the 1800s, the duPonts built gunpowder mills here along the Brandywine. There were frequent explosions. A lot of men died."

Melinda abruptly sat down on the grass and put her face in her hands. Her hair fell in front of her face, and she could feel the dew on the grass soaking through her jeans. The grief she felt for these long-dead souls temporarily blotted out her physical discomfort. She felt a tightness in her chest from the sudden impact of her troubling vision.

"This is something new for me. I'm not used to seeing so many dead people in one place. It's taking the breath right out of me."

Emily knelt next to her.

"Can you see anything else? A battlefield or a building?"

"No, no buildings, no battle taking place, but there is a horrible smell. Gunpowder, I think, and stale blood and festering wounds. I see men walking around, not understanding where they are or what's happened to them. Some are limping; some are bleeding."

Melinda trembled beneath her denim jacket. Emily leaned toward her and put her arm across her shoulders. Sometimes she wished she could share Melinda's visions. Other times, like this one, she was just as glad she could not.

"Wait, there's someone else here now. The men have gone. I see a boy, maybe eight years old. He says his name is Corey. He has brown hair and he's covered with soot. He's crying. Are you looking for your mother...or your father? Just petting the horses? Who? Where? Oh...he's gone."

Melinda came out of her vision, sweat beading on her forehead. Emily hugged her closer. Melinda sat slumped against her quietly for a few moments; then she picked up her head and said, "Let's go find her."

"Her?" Emily asked.

"Yes, her. The girl Corey says is waiting for us."

CHAPTER TWO

The Hawk Watch

The path the women chose climbed a swell of green meadow away from the park office. They passed a wood sign shaped like an arrow that announced "Hawk Watch." They saw no hawks, but invisible birds called "woo-eet" to each other in the still morning air.

As they walked, they passed a low stone wall on their left that continued up the hill for about a hundred yards. The boulders were the size of large pumpkins, stacked together carefully with smaller stones set in between to fill the cracks. Halfway up, there was a six-foot break in the wall; then the stones picked up again for another hundred yards up to the top of the Watch. When they came to the break, Melinda stopped.

"Here," she said. "This is where Corey told me to go. Through the stone fence and over to that fallen tree."

Trampled grass led them about twenty yards to a decaying tree lying on its side. The trunk was smothered in a tangle of leafless vines and dead bushes, but as they examined it, Emily saw a bare foot poking out from under leaves that had been piled on top. Her hand began to shake as she pointed it out to Melinda.

"There?"

They dropped to their knees and hurriedly began to brush away the debris. One bare foot gave way to another bare foot, and two jean-clad legs. Emily noticed red polish on the toes—a woman.

As they clawed away dirt, twigs, and leaves from the form, Melinda murmured, "I hear a howling wind, Em, but I don't see it or feel it," and nothing more.

When they reached the woman's waist, they could see that her white top had been partially pushed up to reveal her lower back, which was covered with the tattoo of an owl. Its wings were extended and reached out almost to her sides. Its body measured four inches high and the wingspan, seven inches. Its eyes were fierce with white pupils, black irises, and gold sclera. Its body and feathers were elaborately colored in gold, black, brown, aqua, and red. Based on all the colors used, Emily knew this was a very expensive tattoo. Whoever this girl was, the tattoo had held great significance for her.

The form's gender was confirmed by lengths of dark blonde hair lying across her back. As they continued to clear away the leaves, they uncovered her head and neck. Her eyes were wide and sightless. Her facial expression was one of surprise. On the neck, they found splotchy red and purple bruises.

"Looks like she was strangled," Melinda suggested, putting her cheek to the woman's slack lips to feel for breath. Finding none, she sat back on her heels.

The scene was almost too awful to comprehend.

For a few moments, Emily thought she might be sick. She kept her eyes averted from the woman's face not wanting to see the grim distortions induced by suffering. She touched the wrist of one tan arm, checking for a pulse. It was creepy cold and still, not like a living thing at all. Melinda made a sign of the cross.

"I don't think we should disturb her any further," Emily suggested. She looked around quickly to see if anyone was watching them, a sudden panic rising in her chest. She had no way of judging how long the girl had been dead. Perhaps there was still someone close by in the woods. After scanning the area in all directions, she was relieved to find no one.

"This woman was obviously murdered, and this is a crime scene," she added. "Let's look around for a purse or something that might tell us who she is."

The two women spent a few moments looking at the ground around the body and beneath the tree. They thrust their hands into the bushes, endured a few scratches, and parted the tall grasses. They found nothing.

"I don't think we should waste any more time on this," Emily said after five minutes. "We need to call the police."

"I agree, but I want to sit here quietly for a few moments to try and contact her spirit. And I want to pray."

Emily was impressed at Melinda's composure. She remembered Melinda's similar equanimity when viewing the corpse of a friend who had drowned just last June. Emily herself was feeling a bit overwhelmed by the horror of this discovery. "You stay here," she decided. "I'll go to the office and ask them to call 9-1-1."

As she walked unsteadily back down the path, Emily wondered who Corey was. Had he been a victim of one of the Eleutherian Mill's accidents? He said he had been petting the horses. As she recalled, in one of the duPont powder mill explosions, all the workers in one building were killed, including the horses hitched to a waiting wagon outside it.

Éleuthère Irénée duPont had opened the gunpowder mills in the early 1800s. The Brandywine River provided the power and immigrants provided the labor.

Although gunpowder was originally made by the Chinese for fireworks, and used with limited success for weapons in Europe, the duPonts had perfected the manufacture of gunpowder with a unique mixture of finely ground saltpeter, sulfur, and charcoal. They sold supplies of gunpowder to the government all through the Civil War, World War I, and World War II.

What made it so effective, however, also made it more volatile. Enormous profits came at the cost of over two hundred lives. The production buildings had been specifically constructed with three stone walls and a fourth wooden wall facing the river, so that when an accident happened, the wooden wall would be blown out first and send the debris, and possibly the workers, into the river.

Halfway to the parking lot, Emily passed a man with tangled black hair and an unshaven face.

They didn't speak, but his scowling mouth gave off a vibe that repelled her, and he smelled of marijuana. A few steps further on she turned around and saw that he had stopped and was staring at Melinda, still sitting with the dead girl. Goosebumps prickled her arms. She waited a few moments to see if he would approach Melinda. When he turned and started walking up the hill again, she thought it was safe to resume her mission.

At the office, Emily was glad to see a young girl at the desk. She looked about twenty-one, with bronzed cheeks and light hair pulled back in a ponytail.

"You need to call 9-1-1," Emily told her. "My friend and I found the body of a young girl up in the Hawk Watch."

"A dead body?" the girl gasped.

"Yes."

The girl shouted for the director, who appeared from a back

office, and repeated what Emily had just told her.

"Show me," said the fiftyish woman with spiked gray hair. She wore the khaki and brown uniform of a Delaware State Park ranger. She went back to her office and grabbed a hat as Emily and the receptionist exchanged questioning looks.

"Call 9-1-1, Denise," the director said as she shepherded Emily out the door.

While they were still on the path back up to where Melinda waited, they heard the sirens. In this ultrawealthy corner of New Castle County, locally referred to as "Chateau Country," help was literally minutes away. Emily and the director turned back around and went down to meet them.

Two New Castle County police officers emerged from a dull brown car: a tall, uniformed African-American man and a shorter Latina woman in civilian dress.

"You called 9-1-1?" the woman asked.

"Yes."

"Where's the body?" asked the man.

"I'll show you," Emily replied and pointed to Melinda who was waving her arms from where she stood at the break in the wall.

The police were quicker than Emily and the director in tackling the climb, and once arriving, they found the two already bent over the dead girl. The woman had two fingers on the girl's neck. Then she looked up at her partner and shook her head "no."

The man used his phone to call for reinforcements, a coroner, and a crime scene unit. The woman shouted down to the ambulance crew that they could leave. When she saw Emily's puzzled expression, she explained that the coroner would use a vehicle from his own office to move the body.

"I'm Detective Lucia Eastlake," the woman now said to them. "And my partner is Officer Winslow. I was consulting with Officer Winslow when the call came in, and I decided to accompany him. How did you happen to find her?"

Detective Eastlake stood only five feet three to Emily's five feet five and Melinda's six feet, but her command of the situation made her seem at least their equal in size.

"We came here for a walk," Emily began. "I parked my car in the lot, we climbed up here, and when we looked through this break in the stone wall, I thought I saw a bare foot. We went over and found the girl lying under the leaves. We moved some of the leaves to see if she were still alive. I checked for a pulse, but otherwise, we didn't touch her. Then I went back down to the park office and asked them to call 9-1-1."

Detective Eastlake wrote down what Emily said in a small notebook. While she was doing this, Emily noticed Officer Winslow returning to the parking lot.

"I'll need your names and addresses," Eastlake said.

Emily gave her their information.

"May I see your ID?"

Emily took out her license and Melinda did likewise.

"These are New Hampshire licenses," Eastlake said. Turning to Emily, she added, "And the address doesn't match the one you gave me."

"I just moved here a few months ago. I haven't gotten around to going to the DMV."

The detective looked questioningly at Melinda.

"I'm visiting and staying at the DoubleTree Hotel in Wilmington."

Eastlake turned back to Emily, "You need to register with the DMV right away."

"I will," Emily promised.

"Do you have a job?"

"Yes, I work for Mirety Bank on Delaware Avenue in Wilmington."

"Never heard of it."

"It used to be Metro Bank until its umpteenth takeover by a Russian conglomerate two months ago.

"What do you do there?"

"I'm a customer service trainer."

"Do you know Carla Delasandro de Garcia?"

"Yes! She's the telephone rep with the pierced eyebrows, right?"

"She's my cousin. I'll ask her if she knows you."

The population of Wilmington, Delaware, is approximately seventy-two thousand. That sounds like a lot of people, but it's more like a small town. Emily didn't know everyone, but there were only two degrees of separation. If you didn't know someone, chances are you knew someone who did.

More sirens were heard, and all turned to watch the crime investigation van enter the parking lot along with another car from the NCCP. Low voices were heard giving instructions as Officer

Winslow directed them up the hill. Six crime scene investigators—three men and three women, wearing identifying vests and carrying cameras and bags of equipment—started the trek up to where the four stood. The last person, in khaki pants and navy windbreaker, still speaking to Officer Winslow, followed them at a distance. When crime scene investigators reached Emily and Melinda, Eastlake directed them to the body.

"Nothing disturbed?" one man asked her.

"Only in discovery," she replied and offered no other observations. Then she turned to the man in civilian dress.

"Detective Smith, these are the two women who found the body."

Emily smiled even though she knew she shouldn't. The grizzled old-timer frowned at her and Melinda. His hair was a bushy brown with spots of gray like a spaniel of some undefinable breed. Emily expected him to pull out a cigarette like the forties' gumshoes, but he didn't.

"Something funny, ma'am?" the detective growled.

"When I was younger, I used to write mystery stories. The detective was always named Smitty."

"Well, I sure ain't him," he replied. "Excuse me while I take a look at the body."

Eastlake accompanied Smith to view the remains of the unfortunate woman while Emily and Melinda kept still and silent, only exchanging glances that communicated "What the hell have we gotten ourselves into this time?"

As they walked to the body, Smith asked Eastlake her assessment of Emily and Melinda. Eastlake said only, "Their shock seems honest and their answers straightforward."

When Detective Smith returned, he said, "Come with me," and started on the path back down to the parking lot.

Once there, he directed Emily and Melinda into the back seat of his car while he took the passenger seat in the front. He found some forms and began to question them for all the same information they'd just given Eastlake. He asked for, and they gave him, their drivers licenses. Each, in turn, repeated their name, address, and how they came to find the body. This time Emily volunteered the reason for the address discrepancy. The detective didn't feel it necessary to admonish her to visit the DMV at her earliest opportunity.

"Did you see anyone else in the vicinity?" he asked.

"As I was walking down to the office I saw a man with dark hair, but he was walking toward me, not away from me."

"Did he speak to you?"

"No."

"Did he do anything suspicious?"

"No."

"Okay," he grunted and continued writing.

Finally, the detective asked them each for a phone number and said he'd be in touch.

After having them sign their statements, he said. "You can go now," adding the classic line, "but don't leave town."

Emily smiled at the cliché, but Melinda frowned.

The detective laughed at her. "Just kidding. Police humor. You can go back to New Hampshire, miss. I have your phone number."

Emily thanked him and fled with Melinda to her own vehicle. As she sat there in the driver's seat, Melinda on the passenger side, Emily noticed that Melinda was trembling slightly. Although dead bodies were routine for the police, they were still a shock for the both of them.

Emily said she'd check the newspaper the next few days to see if the police had learned the girl's name and what had happened to her. Melinda was silent. She didn't need her extra senses to tell her there was violence involved. She put her face in her hands and said another prayer for the poor girl. Emily started the car.

"Let's find some coffee and something to eat," Emily said. "I'm in no mood for a walk."

CHAPTER THREE

THE OWL

As they sat in the Howard Johnson's on the Concord Pike and waited for their order, Melinda took out a pen and tried to recreate the owl tattoo on a white paper napkin.

"Not sure how much I can eat," Emily sighed. "You really liked that tattoo, huh?"

"It might be important. Owls have significance for Native Americans. They represent wisdom and sacred knowledge. Maybe this girl was murdered because of something she knew."

"Tell me more about your vision and the little boy Corey."

"He just appeared, with tears running down his dirty cheeks. He said, 'You have to find the girl under the tree, halfway up the hill, through the hole in the wall. She needs you.'"

"You said something about horses."

"Oh, yes. When I asked him who he was, he said his name was Corey and that he'd been petting the horses when there was an explosion. He was waiting for his father. He's been there looking for his father for a long time. That's how he knew about the girl."

They stopped talking as the waitress brought coffee for Emily, tea for Melinda. Emily had just managed a sip when a man appeared at their table. He was tall, thin, with smooth brown hair and a hawkish nose. His photo-gray sunglasses were still dark from the outside, but she knew him immediately.

"Looky here," he said, removing his shades to reveal piercing brown eyes. "I think it's a flaming-haired Geena Davis and her Hollywood pal Diane Keaton having breakfast in little old Wilmington, Delaware. What brings you two illustrious ladies to our neck of the woods?" Emily smiled at the ridiculousness of his comparisons while Melinda kept her attention on the napkin.

"Hi, Rick. You're out early."

"Just took my mom to church. Now we're here for breakfast." He beamed his best public relations smile and asked Emily point-blank, "Who's your friend?"

"The Geena Davis look-alike is actually my friend, Melinda," she said, nodding her head. "She's visiting me from New Hampshire. Melinda, this is Rick, my boss at the bank."

Melinda picked up her head at this, abandoning her drawing. She just mumbled "Hi" and stared at him. Emily was worried he'd invite himself to eat with them; he was annoying that way, always wanting in on the lives of his employees. She didn't say anything else, hoping he would take the hint and leave.

He did. "Well, I better go find where my mom is sitting. See you tomorrow, Emily."

"Tomorrow," she responded and watched him saunter away down the aisle.

"You don't like him," Melinda observed.

"No. He's very nice to me, almost too nice, but I don't trust him."

"He's attractive enough. He's single I'm guessing, and he's about our age. What's not to like?"

"Yes, to all that, and I did use to like him, but one evening I was working late and I don't think he saw me in my cubicle. His office is maybe twenty feet from mine, and I can't usually hear him when he's in there, but that evening I heard him shouting on the phone to someone.

"It sounded like the switchboard had misrouted a call to him and he was really angry about it. He yelled at the operator for half an hour—half an hour!—to a stranger who had just misdirected a call. When the berating got bad, I thought to check the time just in case this was ever a human resources matter, and I timed him at a full half hour of pouring abuse on this poor person, calling them incompetent, asking who they reported to, and how he was going to have them fired."

"Scary! Can you post out of that department?"

"No. I was lucky enough to get this job rather than be let go when the Delaware and New Hampshire banks merged. I have to wait at least one year to post for a new position. My coping mechanism is to go into survival mode when he's around."

"Survival mode?"

"Head down, mouth shut. No eye contact and keep my opinions to myself."

"Wow, what fun to work at your bank."

"Be grateful for your trust fund and try to make it last. The working world for over-fifty women is not a pretty place."

"His aura was not encouraging either."

"What did you see?" Emily asked. One of the fun things about knowing Melinda was her ability to read auras. She could give you an inside track on someone's personality just by picking up on the subtle colors that flowed around their bodies.

"His was a mix of related colors—pink, orange, and red—but swirling within a muddy brown fog. Very unpleasant."

"What does that mean?"

"That he's dishonest and angry. I agree with you. You're better off treating him like a bad cold. Keep your distance and wash your hands frequently."

"An apt metaphor for the workplace," Emily laughed.

When their breakfast arrived, the women managed to eat only half their pancakes. Melinda kept fiddling with her drawing of the owl.

"I'm going to research this while you're at work tomorrow," she said. "Do you mind?"

"Of course not. Are you going to see Elvis this afternoon?"

Melinda had met Elvis on a cruise she had taken with Emily in June. The stars were smiling when it turned out that he lived in Emily's hometown of Wilmington, Delaware.

"Yes, he's picking me up at the hotel at noon. He's going to cook dinner for me tonight. I'm a little nervous."

"Preflight jitters," Emily teased. "By the way, when does your plane leave for Manchester?" Emily picked up her purse to leave.

"Tuesday at 8 a.m. Don't worry about driving me to the airport. The hotel has a shuttle. Dinner tomorrow night still okay?"

"Sure. I'll call around four tomorrow afternoon, and we can discuss what time to meet you and Elvis for dinner."

"Hopefully I'll have some news for you about the owl."

"Sounds good. Let's go."

Emily drove Melinda back to her hotel and hugged her good-bye. Then she headed south to rural Odessa where Desmond's house was located. She parked her car in the driveway and found him seated on the back porch with a book and a glass of bourbon over ice. It seemed a little early in the day for drinking, but she didn't mention it. She checked out his book and saw that it was an old Dickens' classic, *Great Expectations*. One of the things she found so attractive about him was his love of reading. Of all the men she dated both before and after being divorced, he was the only one who read something other than *Penthouse* and *Time* magazines.

"Did your laundry," he said. "It's folded and on your bed."

"You went in my room?"

"Sure, why not? It's my house."

"Okay…well…thank you. But you know I'm perfectly capable of doing my own laundry."

"Sure, but the machine's old. I'm afraid you'll overload it or use too much detergent. I'm happy to do it for you."

Emily sighed. He didn't ask her to join him or offer to get her a drink.

"I'll be in the TV room upstairs," she said to him after a pause. "See you later."

Having some time on her hands and not much to do, Emily decided to call her old friends, Janet and Sue, whom she had met twenty-plus years ago while working a second job at JCPenney's during Christmas. The three women, being the only three under sixty-five at that time working in the Housewares department, formed a quick bond. When the Christmas season had passed they'd stayed friends, going out for drinks on the weekend and calling each other with boyfriend troubles, or engagement announcements, and later new baby and new home news.

Even in New Hampshire, Emily had kept in touch with them, and they had been her lifeline through the heartbreak of her divorce and the lonely years following it. Although they weren't there to commiserate with over a glass of wine, the sympathetic voice of one or the other on the telephone line was often all that stood between a night of peaceful rest or a night of sobbing herself to sleep.

When she had been transferred back to Delaware, she looked forward to renewing these old friendships in person. In an odd quirk of fate, however, she found that these relationships, which she had so carefully nurtured during her years in New Hampshire, seemed to unravel when she returned to Wilmington. Janet and Sue were still available to talk on the phone, but when she tried to plan a weekend coffee or lunch date, one always had a church meeting, or the other was babysitting grandchildren. Some days Emily wondered if her being single and childless left them with too little in common. She never minded hearing about arguments with their spouses or the achievements of their children, but she often got the vibe that her trials and tribulations of dating or her bouts of loneliness were considered trivial compared to their family dramas.

On this particular Sunday afternoon, when Emily tried to contact first one and then the other, she learned that Janet was at the gym and Sue was putting in overtime at the office.

Emily turned on the TV and found a Philadelphia Eagles football game. Donovan McNabb was making coach Andy Reid and the Philadelphia fans proud. Her first husband had been a rabid follower, often explaining to friends that his religion was "The Church of NFL Football." Consequently, Emily had become proficient in first down attempts and third down strategies. She settled in to enjoy the game.

CHAPTER FOUR

ALICIA

The next morning, when Emily arrived at work, she parked her car on the seventh level of the parking garage. She loved the convenience of this spot. She had been allotted a space near the door and had only a few yards to traverse to enter the building and then take an elevator to her office on the tenth floor. The first floor of the building held a branch office for Mirety's commercial banking, offices for their mortgage business, and the security command center. Levels two through seven were designated for parking. Then more banking offices and executive suites completed the fourteen-story edifice. The basement housed a cafeteria and supply rooms.

Emily had barely sat down and booted up her PC when her fellow trainer, Kathy, arrived and propped her elbows on the cubicle wall. Kathy was just a few years younger than Emily but had been working at this location under three different bank ownerships over the past ten years. She was confident and savvy, with sharply angled black hair and a runway model's figure draped in classic suits and real gold accessories. She always knew "the skinny" before anyone else did. She belonged in a forties movie seated next to Lauren Bacall with a cigarette in one hand and a martini in the other. She'd quit smoking, but she did love a vodka martini.

"Got news," she said. "One of our customer service reps was murdered this weekend."

"What! Who? One of my trainees?"

"No. Her name's Alicia Kingston. She'd been here a while. Here's the news story."

Kathy handed her the front section of the *Wilmington Reporter*. The headlines ran "Young Girl Murdered in Brandywine Creek State Park." Included was a high school graduation photo of the girl Emily and Melinda had discovered the day before.

Emily scanned the article to see if her name was included in the story, but it only said the girl had been found by two women walking in the park. It confirmed what Kathy had relayed: that the girl's name was Alicia Kingston, and she was twenty-four years old. Here was the face that Emily and Melinda had been unable to appreciate: full cheeks, large eyes, and a wide smile that was just a tad lopsided in the perfectly oval countenance. *Thank goodness it doesn't mention me,* Emily thought. If the girl worked here at the bank, the higher-ups might think she had something to do with it.

"Don't tell anyone," she said to Kathy, "but I found her. That is, my friend Melinda and I found her. We're the two women mentioned in the story. I had no idea she worked here."

"No way! She not only worked here, but she used to date our illustrious boss. They split; she dated around; and then she got engaged to our admin, Howdy. She was quite the confused chickee. Have the police questioned you?"

"Just yesterday when they arrived at the scene."

"How did she look?"

"Horrible. Cold and lifeless."

"It says she was strangled. They're asking for anyone with information to contact them."

"I wonder what she was doing up there Saturday night. It's not that warm in October."

"Probably watching the meteor shower."

"Explain."

"You don't know about the Draconids? That's a meteor shower that arrives every October. Brandywine Creek State Park is one of the best viewing areas around here because you're far enough away from the city lights to see the meteors falling."

"I wonder if she was watching the meteor shower when she was killed. Oh, the poor girl."

Emily had to pause as her mind envisioned the trusting young woman, lying on her back in the soft grass, filled with wonder as she watched the meteors fall in swooping white arcs across the dark sky. At what point did her awe turn to terror? When were all the possible beauties of the universe snuffed out by the horror of death?

"Well, I told the police where I work," Emily continued. "I'm sure I'll be hearing from them."

"I wouldn't say anything about it to our boss, Mr. Rick Wiseass."

"Wiseburg."

"I like my name for him. Let me know if you need me to cover any of your training classes. I have a light week."

"Thanks, Kath. Talk to you later."

.

CHAPTER FIVE

The Boyfriend

Howdy sat rigidly on the straight-backed metal chair. His stiff muscles ached anywhere they made contact with the chair, as if it were a medieval torture device. His lower back was seething, his thighs on the verge of convulsing. He uncrossed and recrossed his legs for the umpteenth time and still found no relief. He'd been left alone to suffer in solitude for thirty minutes now. He looked around the room, then up at the ceiling corners. He saw the camera. He knew people were watching him. He splayed his elbows on the gray metal table and lowered his face into his open hands. He didn't know how much more of this he could take.

Finally, a female detective opened the door, walked in, and sat down opposite him. She said, "Good morning, Mr. Evans. I'm Detective Eastlake."

Howdy was startled by the young brunette who confidently pulled out the chair opposite him and sat down with the authority of one who had done this a hundred times before. The door opened again, and an older man joined her.

"This is Detective Smith," she continued. "We have a few questions for you."

Howdy was too frightened to respond. He sat silently as the second detective seated himself and fixed his eyes on him. Howdy was truly terrified.

Neither detective smiled as if pretending this were a pleasant social visit. Nor did they frown as if they'd already decided upon his guilt. They merely sat with stone faces and observed him. They continued to sit silently staring at him for an agonizing five minutes, saying nothing. This tactic was one of their favorite methods of intimidation.

They examined the slightly built young man with splotchy skin and carrot hair. Eastlake, often concerned about her own weight, pegged him at one hundred and thirty pounds. That would make him ten pounds less than herself. She could easily take him in a fight. Smith was more concerned with the young man's slenderness. He had the eyes of a frightened rabbit, and if one didn't hold onto him tightly, he could easily squirm away. Not that there was anywhere he could go. Smith just liked to be prepared.

Finally, Eastlake turned to a small tape recorder sitting on the table and pushed the "Record" button. She gave the date, the time, the location, and who was in the room.

"Please state your name for the record," Eastlake said to Howdy.

"Howard Aloysius Evans."

"And your address?"

"I'm at 9597 West Eighteenth Street, Wilmington, Delaware."

"Your employer?"

"Mirety Bank on Delaware Avenue."

"I understand that Alicia Kingston was your girlfriend, correct?" she queried.

"Yes," Howdy responded, dropping his voice to a whisper.

"Were you two engaged to be married?"

"Sort of."

"What does 'sort of' mean?" Smith asked.

"It wasn't official. I hadn't bought a ring. We hadn't set a date."

"But your friends and coworkers knew you were getting married, right?" Eastlake asked.

"Mostly, yeah." He squirmed here. The detectives took note.

"When was the last time you saw Alicia?" Smith this time.

"Friday at work."

"You didn't see her Saturday? No weekend plans?" Back to Eastlake.

"I wasn't feeling well. I have terrible allergies, especially in the spring and fall. I'd taken some pills and they made me sleepy, so I stayed in on Saturday. I especially can't go outdoors when the leaves are dying and they're all moldy on the ground."

"Can anyone testify that they saw you or spoke to you at home?" Smith asked.

"I talked to my boss, Rick Wiseburg. He called around five."

"And what did you two talk about?" Eastlake asked.

"Work, mostly. You can ask him." The back and forth between the two detectives was beginning to rattle Howdy. He looked from one to the other and back again. Trying to anticipate each question.

"We will. And you didn't go out all evening?" Smith asked.

"No." Howdy twisted around, recrossing his legs. "Should I get a lawyer?"

"No need," Eastlake said. "We're almost done."

"Can you think of anyone who would want to hurt Alicia?" Smith asked.

Howdy had anticipated this routine question. He knew that as the boyfriend he was the prime suspect.

"Her brother has been living with her, and she'd recently told him to move out. She was tired of supporting him. He doesn't have a job. I imagine he's not too happy."

"Did he say anything to you personally about this?" Eastlake asked.

"No."

"Thank you for your time, Mr. Evans," Smith said. "We'll be in touch."

CHAPTER SIX

THE POLICE

The police did call—specifically Detective Lucia Eastlake—late that Monday morning, and Emily took a long lunch hour to make the short drive to the New Castle County Department of Public Safety, south of Wilmington, on US Route 13, also known as the duPont Highway. The ninety-seven-mile-long highway stretching the length of Delaware had been built as a philanthropic effort by T. Coleman duPont in 1911 with groundbreaking at the Delaware-Maryland line. His hope was that this connecting roadway would be an economic boon to the farmers in rural Sussex County.

The highway was completed in 1923, and in 1934 it was expanded between Wilmington and Dover to become the first divided highway in the nation. The New Castle County Department of Public Safety was located on the eastern or northbound side of the highway where it bisected Minquadale. Emily had no problem locating the curved glass structure that on this sunny day was reflecting a darkish blue sky.

There were several female detectives at the front desk, and one escorted her down freshly painted tan hallways to Detective Eastlake's desk. The detective was eating her lunch from a plastic salad container.

She asked Emily all the same questions she and Smith had asked previously and had her sign a typewritten statement, noting that there'd been no change. Emily said she'd seen the newspaper story and thanked her for keeping her name out of it.

"Oh, that's protocol," Eastlake explained. "Whoever killed this girl might think you saw something and target you."

"Oh! I never thought of that."

"Think about it. Do you live alone?"

"I rent a room in a house with a man about my age. I've known him since high school. I feel safe there."

"Good, but let us know if anyone follows you, or if some stranger contacts you asking for information."

"I will."

"This girl worked where you work. Did you know her?"

"No, I've only been there a few months. I work with new hires, so I don't meet a lot of other employees outside of training."

"What do you train them to do?"

"Be customer service reps. They answer the phone and help the corporate customers."

"Checking accounts or credit cards?"

"Our department handles large business accounts, companies with five hundred or more employees. Most calls involve payroll, monthly statements, and wire transfers. I train them to navigate a complicated system where they use multiple software programs to investigate problems and coordinate with other branches of the bank if needed. It's not easy. The callers are usually members of their company's Treasury department. They're very detail oriented and anxious not to make mistakes."

"Could she have been the target of an irate customer or jealous coworker?"

"I don't know, but you could speak to her immediate supervisor or her manager. He's the same man I report to, Rick Wiseburg." Emily gave her his phone number.

"You have the same boss and you don't know Alicia Kingston?"

"It's a big department—maybe sixty customer service reps, four supervisors, two trainers, and two administrative assistants. I'm rarely on the floor. I'm mostly in the training classroom or at my desk."

"Okay. We'll be in touch if there are any more questions."

"Can you tell me anything more about how she died? The paper only said that she was strangled."

"That's all we know for now. We're looking at friends and family. If you don't see anything more in the paper, give me a call. I'll update you."

"Thanks. I will."

When Emily returned to work, Rick was waiting, seated in her chair with his feet on her desk.

"You're a little late."

"Just a few minutes. Did you need me for something?" She

didn't want to explain where she'd been. If he knew, he would probably pump her for information, and she really didn't have any. Why create a situation where she would only be at a disadvantage?

"Have you heard about Alicia Kingston's murder? She was one of our customer service reps."

"Oh, yes, I did hear." She left it at that.

"Have you heard any scuttlebutt about who did it? Any gossip on the floor?"

"I'm afraid I haven't talked to any of the reps today."

"Well, if you hear anything, let me know, okay?"

"Sure."

Rick removed his brogans from her work space and jumped to his feet.

"Tell me right away, got it?" and he strode off back to his office. Emily wondered if there was any connection between Rick's appearance at the diner and his questioning her today. It left her feeling slightly ill. She decided to skip lunch.

CHAPTER SEVEN

GINA

Wanting to know more about the poor woman whose mysterious death she was now a part of, Emily decided to pay a visit to the Customer Service floor and see the cubicle where Alicia had worked. It wasn't unusual for a trainer to spend time with the representatives who were on the phone, so her appearance wouldn't seem amiss.

She took the elevator down to the eighth floor and began to walk up and down the aisles of cubicles where approximately forty reps were currently on the phone. At three in the afternoon, another group would arrive to work until eleven. The Wilmington site handled calls for North America, so this schedule provided coverage up until 8 p.m. on the West Coast.

All the cubes had nameplates on their exterior side walls, but Emily didn't need to look for a name. Alicia's desk was already a shrine covered with bouquets of carnations intermingled with baby's breath, small stuffed animals, balloons, and sympathy cards. Her heart sank as she noticed a photo of a boyfriend. In fact, on closer inspection, she recognized the man in the picture of the young couple with their heads tilted and touching, happy grins on their faces. Alicia's boyfriend was none other than Howdy Evans, one of Training's administrative assistants. Kathy had told her they were engaged, but Emily had found it hard to believe that a beautiful girl such as Alicia was engaged to the lackluster admin with red hair and freckles.

The rep in the next cube appeared to be watching her. After a moment, she took off her headset and said to Emily, "Are you looking for Alicia? I'm afraid she's gone…I mean she's passed…I'm sorry, what I'm trying to say and can't seem to get out is that she's dead. She was murdered over the weekend. It's awful. You can read about it in this morning's paper."

"Oh, I'm so sorry to hear that." Emily thought fast for a cover story. "I was told she could lend me a book I wanted to read."

"You should talk to her friend Gina. She works on the first floor in Mortgages. Although she may have taken the day off because of what happened to Alicia."

"Thank you. I'll go find her."

Emily walked away, wondering about Howdy Evans. She hadn't seen him so far today, but then she'd either been busy on her computer or with Detective Eastlake at the police station. Then she realized that, of course, he would be out on compassionate leave.

She took the elevator to the first floor, entered the Mortgages front office, and walked up to the receptionist. "I'm looking for Gina in Mortgages. I don't know her last name."

"Her office is back there," she said, waving toward the rear of the building. "She's in, but she's not feeling well today."

"Don't worry. I won't be long."

Emily found Gina's office easy enough and saw a thirtyish blonde woman with straight hair and sad brown eyes sitting at a mahogany desk. Even a stranger could tell she was looking at her PC screen without seeing what was on it. She had a sad, faraway expression on her face, mentally visiting her own haunting world of grief.

"Gina, I'm sorry to bother you," Emily said as she approached.

Gina jerked upright at Emily's voice. "Oh, no bother," she managed. "I'm just distracted right now."

"My name is Emily Menotti. I'm a trainer up on the tenth floor. I was so sorry to hear about Alicia Kingston. She was your friend, right?"

"Yes. Did you know her?"

"No, not personally, but I know she died over the weekend."

"Oh, you know? Isn't it horrible? Why would anyone want to hurt her?"

"I've no idea. But I wanted to tell you that I was the one who found her body."

"You did? How?"

"I was walking in the park with my friend. We saw her foot sticking out from under some leaves and called the police."

"How did she look? Was she beaten up? Oh, I hate to think of what she might have suffered. Oh, oh…" Gina tilted her head toward her desk and grabbed a Kleenex to staunch tears.

Emily sat down in the customer's chair in front of the desk. As she did, an older man interrupted them and walked past Emily, seeming not to notice her.

"Good job Friday," his voice boomed out in the small room. He had longish gray hair and a sizable gut spilling over his suit trousers.

"This should cheer you up," he said as he placed a folded piece of notepaper on her desk. Peeking out from its folds was a one-hundred-dollar bill. In a reflection of his grooming skills, he'd done a sloppy job of concealing it.

"That's for the mortgage applications you submitted last week and all your hard work." Then as suddenly as he had blustered in, he was gone.

"Wow, I wish my boss would do that," Emily lowered her head and whispered.

"He's not supposed to if someone else is here," Gina said, grabbing the notepaper and shoving it in a desk drawer.

"It's an incentive program they're running right now. Five applications in one week and you get one hundred dollars. Then you get fifty dollars for each one that's approved. Best of all it's in cash, so I don't have to report it."

"Is that legal?"

"Who knows? If the bosses don't care, I certainly don't."

"Maybe I should switch jobs. Do you take a lot of mortgage applications?"

"About six or seven a week."

"How many get approved?"

"Most of them. It's easier to get a mortgage now than it's ever been. Pretty much anyone with a paycheck can get a hundred thousand. A married couple with two incomes can get two hundred thousand."

"I assume you check their credit report."

"Most of the time. If they state that they have a good income, and good assets, they don't even have to provide pay stubs."

"Wow! That sounds risky. How many default?"

"Not my department," she smiled. "The gimmick is to collect that two-hundred-dollar mortgage application fee. After approval, someone else worries about whether they actually make the payments. And by that time, we've bundled the mortgages up and sold them to some other bank. Don't tell anyone, but there are whole communities where Mirety provided the new construction funding, and then, later, more than fifty percent went into default. But by that time, they were somebody else's problem."

"Sounds like poor business practices to me. But that's not why I stopped by to see you. What I want to know is if you had any idea why someone would kill your friend. I work with Howdy Evans. Is he her boyfriend? Do you think he would hurt her?"

"Oh god, no. He's a pussycat. He doted on her. I really can't think of any reason someone would do this."

"Did she have family in the area?"

"Just a brother. Her parents died when she was eighteen. She never mentioned an aunt or uncle. She and her brother often spent Christmas at my house."

Gina's grief had abated now. She ran her fingers through her hair and shook her head to adjust her mood, which conveyed the message that it was time for her to get back to work. Emily took the hint.

"I've got to go," she said. "I'm going to follow the police investigation to see if they find Alicia's killer. If I have any news, I'll let you know."

"Thank you, Emily.

After work, Emily met Melinda and Elvis for dinner in the DoubleTree hotel restaurant. They drank wine and enjoyed broiled steaks. Emily was happy to see the couple sitting cozily together, laughing at each other's jokes, and spinning out that delicious web of love and romance that Emily didn't see much these days. If things worked out, perhaps Melinda would relocate to Wilmington and Emily could see her more often. She had become Emily's best friend when Emily lived in New Hampshire. Her absence was an unwelcome hole in Emily's life in Wilmington.

"Oh, I almost forgot to tell you," Melinda said over cheesecake and coffee. "About that owl tattoo on the girl we found...I couldn't find that particular one having any significance.

"There's a group called the Order of the Owls that began in South Bend, Indiana, as a service organization, but their owl insignia is very different. There's an Order of the Owl heavy metal band in Atlanta, Georgia, but they also use a different logo. There's an award called the Order of the Owl in the construction sciences, but that's just a piece of paper. I couldn't find anything that looked like that tattoo. It has a Native American look. I'll do more research when I get home."

Emily filled her in on everything she'd found out so far which, aside from Alicia working at her bank and being engaged to Howdy, didn't amount to much.

"So sad," Elvis commented. "Will you follow up with the police?"

"Of course. I feel attached to her somehow, like she's my responsibility. I'll ask around the bank some more and see what I can find out."

"Have you seen your family since you've been back in Delaware?" Melinda asked, changing the subject.

"No, I haven't. I called my sister one day, but she was busy with customers. You know she has a bake shop in Rehoboth, right?"

"Yes, and your brothers both work downstate too?"

"Yes, one's in real estate, and the other runs a small restaurant with his wife. They're all entrepreneurs. I don't know what happened to me. Didn't inherit those do-it-yourself genes."

"Will you get down to see them?" Elvis asked.

"One of these days, maybe in the spring when the weather's nice. I love to walk on the beach. What about you? Are you a beach person?" she asked Elvis.

"My family has a cottage in Dewey." He turned to Melinda and explained, "That's a funky little place just south of Rehoboth that the locals are perpetually trying to reclaim from the college kids who trash it each summer. We'll have to go there sometime."

"You have to go into Rehoboth, though, to get caramel corn at Dolle's," Emily said.

"And go to Lewes for ice cream at King's," Elvis added.

"I'm feeling fat already," Melinda laughed.

"You'll dance it off at night in Ocean City, Maryland," Emily said, "but I'm totally out of touch with what the good clubs are now. It's been over ten years since I've been there. I'm guessing Fager's Island and Secrets are still there. My ex and I used to sneak around the side of the parking lot onto the back deck of Fager's Island to avoid the cover charge."

"Not you, Miss Goody Two Shoes!" Melinda teased.

"We were perpetually broke. It was a very upscale place. But they always had the best dance music."

"We'll check them all out this summer. Me with two women, one on each arm. I can't wait," Elvis said.

"Don't get ahead of yourself, Casanova," Melinda said punching him lightly on the arm, but she was grinning. Emily couldn't remember if she'd ever seen her so happy.

"Have a good flight tomorrow," Emily told her as she rose to leave. "Give me a call tomorrow night, okay?"

"Will do." After hugs all around, Emily left Melinda in Elvis's loving hands.

When she arrived at Desmond's house thirty minutes later, she found him already asleep in his porch chair, his book in his lap, and an empty glass near his hand. She turned off the porch light and left him to his slumber.

CHAPTER EIGHT

The Brother

Greg Kingston had lost his parents four years ago. He'd lost his job nine months ago. He'd had his home foreclosed six months after losing his job. Now his sister was dead. On Sunday afternoon he'd identified her body at the morgue in the Medical Examiner's Unit. About the only thing of substance he had left to his name was a rusting VW microbus that he had driven to police headquarters to keep the appointment with Detectives Smith and Eastlake.

Greg moved restlessly on the cold metal chair. He had already figured out that the room's furnishings and the long wait were all strategies to make the person waiting uncomfortable and, perhaps, even eager to confess to anything in order to be allowed to leave.

Greg himself was not worried or in a hurry. He was unemployed, so there was no place else he needed to be. He did wish they'd turn up the heat as his Metallica tee shirt and thin jeans weren't sufficient to keep him warm in the chilly room. He ran his fingers repeatedly through light brown hair that shone greasily in the yellow fluorescent lighting.

"We're very sorry for your loss," Detective Eastlake began when the two finally entered the room, introduced themselves, and started the recording equipment. "We're hoping you can help us find whoever killed your sister."

"I'll answer any questions you have, but I really can't think of anyone who would want to hurt her."

"When was the last time you saw your sister?" Detective Smith asked.

"Saturday afternoon. I've been staying with her since I lost my house. I went out with friends in the afternoon, and she was home. She told me she was planning to see the meteor shower at Brandywine Creek State Park that night."

"Who was she going with?" Eastlake asked.

"I didn't ask. I just assumed her boyfriend, Howdy."

"Howdy said he was sick and didn't go. Would she have gone by herself?" Smith wanted to know.

"Sure. She was all excited about seeing the Draconids. She said that, in mystical lore, meteor showers were an opportunity for rebirth—that cosmic events illuminate new paths and give a person's life renewed meaning."

"We didn't find her car at the park." Eastlake pointed out.

"Oh well, who knows. Maybe, when Howdy canceled, she talked another friend into going with her."

"But not you?" This question came from Smith.

"Not me."

"Where were you Saturday night?" asked Eastlake.

"Hanging out at Alicia's. Watching TV."

"Can anyone vouch for you?" Again from Smith.

"No, I'm afraid not."

The two detectives leaned back in their chairs and looked at each other. Greg was sitting with his legs and arms crossed but otherwise at ease. He wasn't fidgeting or glancing around the room as if searching for answers. Who to believe? It was early days. These were informal sessions. They were poking around trying to decide which were the best leads to invest their too little time and not enough money in.

"You can go," Smith finally said. "We'll be in touch."

"Let me know before it's in the papers, will you? I don't want to find out who killed my sister on the six o'clock news."

"Will do," Eastlake mumbled. Greg gratefully rose and fled as quickly as common sense allowed.

CHAPTER NINE
LUNCH AND DINNER

On Thursday morning, as Emily was reviewing updated information to include in her next training class, Rick Wiseburg stopped by her desk. He looked especially spiffy that day, in a soft gray wool suit with a pink handkerchief that matched his tie.

"We're having a lunch meeting at the Greenery at noon," he said. "Can you be there?"

"Of course."

When Emily arrived five minutes early at the restaurant, which was on the first floor of an office building not far from theirs, she was surprised to see Howdy sitting at the table.

"Didn't expect to see you," Emily said. "I'm so sorry about Alicia. Is the date set for her funeral?"

"Yes, next Monday, with a viewing Sunday afternoon. Will you come?"

"I can make the viewing, but I don't feel that I knew her well enough to ask off for the funeral. Did you know that I was the one who found her?"

"Yes, Gina told me. Uh-oh, here comes Rick." Howdy stood up.

Rick nodded at Emily briefly and grasped Howdy's hand. "I'm so sorry," he said. "Thank you for coming in today. We have a lot to discuss and I needed you to be here."

"No problem," Howdy replied as they all sat down. Within a few seconds, the other trainer, Kathy, and the other administrative assistant, Nora Weatherly, joined them. Twenty-five and single, Howdy had no ex-wives and no children. He projected a sense of unease with himself and with others. Unfortunately, Howdy's red hair had earned him the nickname of Howdy Doody among some of the older staff, but he took it good-naturedly. Many of his colleagues were too young to remember the puppet friend of

Buffalo Bob Smith. Emily and Kathy, who were old enough, kindly refrained from using the nickname.

Nora was older than all of them, closing in on retirement, but because she was divorced, she needed to work. She took a mother hen attitude toward them all. Even here in the restaurant, she had sat down and made a show of opening her napkin, placing it in her lap, smoothing it carefully so that it covered her skirt, and then looking around the table at them all as if to say "Now children, follow my example."

Rick ordered a bottle of red wine while they all silently studied the menu. After the wine arrived, Rick asked who would like a drink. The women all declined. Emily didn't trust Rick; he could offer wine one day and then use it as a demerit on her yearly performance review.

Howdy accepted the drink, and Rick smiled affectionately at him—a smile Emily caught, but she thought the others had missed. What was that about? She had to wonder.

The waitress took their orders, with the women in agreement once again with requests for salad platters, while the men ordered steak and French fries. When the waitress left, there was an uncomfortable silence. No one seemed to know why they were there.

After thirty awkward seconds, Rick broke the silence. "Our meeting will come to order. The first item of business is the death of our colleague, Alicia Kingston. Nora, will you send flowers to the funeral home from our department?"

"Yes. Howdy, can you get me the address?"

"I'll have it for you when we get back."

"Next order of business," Rick continued, "the rumor that there is an organization intent on disrupting the bank. Have you all heard about it?"

Everyone sat up, surprised. They shook their heads. No, they hadn't.

"You all saw the movie *Fight Club*?"

Again, heads shook in the negative, except Howdy's and Emily's.

"I've seen it," Howdy said. "Pretty violent. They have this crazy idea that, by blowing up banks, everyone's credit card debt will be erased."

"Guess none of them work in banking," Kathy offered. "Or else they'd know we back up everything on our computers. If you want to do real damage, you'd need to attack the backups."

Rick broke in, "Yes, yes, but there are other reasons to disrupt banking. As you know, per recent legislation, banks can now merge with insurance companies and offer those products and services. My friends upstairs tell me Mirety is looking at Corponium Insurance. If we merge with them, we'll not only be one of the largest international banks but also the largest insurance underwriter in the world." He paused to let this sink in.

"However, Corponium is not well liked in the Middle East. They've underwritten the businesses of several oil-wealthy sheiks. As a result, Corponium has been the victim of numerous terrorist attacks in Britain and France. I'm guessing the terrorists could turn their sights on Mirety Bank here in the US as well."

Emily sighed. *Just what I needed. Something else to worry about.*

"What do you want us to do?" Howdy asked.

"Keep your eyes and ears open. If you hear any rumors on the floor about a disgruntled employee or a threatening phone call, please let me know right away." He gave Howdy an intense stare as if trying to convey something else besides alarm, maybe a personal message of concern. Then he sipped his wine.

Howdy raised his own glass and met Rick's gaze. Emily's stomach did a flip-flop. What was going on?

"Have there been any incidents we should know about?" Kathy asked, accepting her plate of greens from a server.

"So far, no," Rick responded. "But that's what worries me."

Emily had to stifle a smile. She remembered a pest control salesman using the exact line with the same reasoning when inspecting her rental home in New Hampshire. We should be more frightened of what we can't see than what we can see was the way this psychological ploy went.

With food on the table, everyone appeared more interested in eating than in hearing about what had Rick worried. And Rick, content to have stirred up everyone's fears, now addressed his empty stomach. No more was said about terrorists, and Emily was glad of that.

When she returned home from work that evening, Desmond was in the kitchen fixing spaghetti and red sauce.

"Want some?" he asked.

"I'd love some. Let me run upstairs and change."

When she got to her room, she noticed that the things on her dresser had been moved around. Had Desmond dusted her room? Or had he been snooping?

When she returned to the kitchen, she asked him, "I noticed my bureau was dusted. Did you do that? You don't have to."

She took a seat as he replied, "It was no bother. I'm allergic to dust so I try to keep everything as dust-free as possible."

"You haven't done it before. I've been here a few months."

"Well, it's fall now, and my seasonal allergies are kicking in, so I try to keep the house especially allergen free. Sorry if my OCD bothers you."

"Oh no, it's okay. I understand. I have allergies also."

He placed a large bowl of pasta, sauce, and broccoli in front of her.

"Uh, Desmond, I don't care for broccoli."

"Oh, come on. It's so good for you. It fights cancer."

"I just don't like the taste." She started to shove the bowl away.

"Please, for me?' he pushed the bowl back toward her. "The taste is very mild. Just try it. And let me give you a glass of wine to wash it down with."

"Well, okay." She knew she should eat more vegetables, but she just didn't care for them.

She tried a bit of the broccoli. Well, it wasn't too bad. If she covered it with red sauce, chewed it quickly, and swallowed it, she could do it. And it was sweet of Desmond to care about her health.

The tart Chianti he poured did help the broccoli go down. The red sauce was savory and hot, the pasta thick and comforting. Desmond brought his own large bowl to the table and joined her. They were quiet as they ate. When the meal was over, she thanked him.

"Will you let me fix you broccoli with your pasta from now on?" he asked.

"Yes, I'd love that." The warmth of the food and wine nudged her heart a bit closer to resurrecting all the passionate feelings she'd had for Desmond once upon a time. Good food, good company, what more could she really want?

CHAPTER TEN

The Diary

On Friday, Emily called Detective Eastlake for an update. The detective wasn't in, but she called back shortly before twelve.

"Can you meet me at Rodney Square at noon? I have some appointments downtown, and I'll be grabbing a quick sandwich from the deli on Market Street. I'll bring you up-to-date."

Located a short walk from the bank building, the Square was a tidy one-block park bordered on the north side by the US Post Office, on the east by the courthouse, on the south by the Wilmington Library, and on the west by the duPont Building, home to the duPont Hotel and The Playhouse. The square itself was graced by a statue of Caesar Rodney, who had been a Continental congressman and signer of the Declaration of Independence.

On her way downtown, Emily stopped at a coffee shop for a cup of hot chocolate to go. Arriving at Rodney Square, she waited only minutes for the detective, who arrived carrying a plastic soda cup and a white paper bundle that held her sandwich.

"How are you?" Eastlake asked as she walked toward Emily and sat down next to her on a low cement wall not far from the statue of Caesar Rodney astride his horse, captured in bronze by the sculptor James E. Kelley.

"Still thinking about Alicia and her tattoo," Emily responded. "Have you found her killer?"

"No, but we've made some progress. We've interviewed those close to her. No clear suspect has emerged. However, we did find her diary, and it seems she was very unhappy at her job. You worked with her, right?"

"Not exactly. I'm a trainer in that department. I've only been there a few months, and I don't remember seeing her around. She wasn't in any of my training classes, but then I only meet new hires."

"And your manager is Rick Wiseburg?"

"Yes."

"And one of the administrative assistants is Howdy Evans?"

"Yes."

"Can you tell me anything about them?"

"Can I ask why?" Emily knew why, but she was hoping to learn something new.

"It's just an avenue of inquiry. It doesn't mean they're suspects."

"Howdy was Alicia's boyfriend. You know that, right?"

"Yes, but he seems very friendly with Mr. Wiseburg also."

"I wouldn't know about that."

"Are you aware of Mr. Wiseburg's reputation?"

Emily felt uncomfortable. She had her suspicions, but that's all they were. She said nothing.

The detective continued. "We've had a few complaints from women who claim he's stalked them. None ever went so far as to press charges. What's odd is that we've had a few complaints from young men also. I think your boss swings both ways. You've never noticed anything at work?"

Emily thought about the looks exchanged between Rick and Howdy. Perhaps there was a personal relationship there. However, she didn't feel sure enough to mention it. Her philosophy was that intimate relationships among consenting adults, whether heterosexual or homosexual, were none of her business. What she answered was "No."

They sat quietly for five minutes while the detective ate her lunch and Emily sipped her hot chocolate. Finally, Emily broke the silence.

"Do you know what the significance of the owl tattoo is?"

"I just took it for a tramp stamp," Eastlake said. "Do you have any other information?"

"No." Again, Emily kept what she'd learned to herself. She didn't see how explaining what the owl *wasn't* a symbol of would help.

Detective Eastlake pulled some pages from her back pocket and smoothed them out on the cement surface.

"Here's a copy of part of her diary, written shortly before her death. It's about her job at the bank. Please read this and let me know what you think. You're an employee and a trainer for her department. Perhaps there's a clue in here that I'm not recognizing."

Emily took the pages and glanced at them briefly. Detective Eastlake rose to leave.

"I'll keep you updated," Eastlake said. With this, she balled up her sandwich wrapper and stuffed it inside the now empty plastic cup.

"Ciao" was all she added, as she walked away down Market Street and tossed the remains of her lunch into a trash can. Emily looked at Alicia's photocopied handwriting and began to read:

Wednesday, October 2, 2000, 3:40 a.m.

I can't sleep. Problems at work are bothering me. I have been at this job for over a year, and it's the unhappiest I have ever been in my career. I read a Dilbert cartoon yesterday about an employee complaining that he doesn't like his job, and Dilbert says, "No one does. That's why they have to pay you to do it." So true, but so little comfort.

In the past, the bad jobs I've had usually become bearable at some point. At this job, though, the problems never seem to let up and people refuse to help you. Oh, they pretend to. They take your question and start to answer, but they don't put their phones in After Call Work, so of course, they get a customer call before they're finished telling you the answer, and then you have no choice but to walk away while they talk to their caller.

Let me back up. I work in a phone shop, Mirety Bank Corporate Customer Service, where the clients are corporations and the callers are usually entry-level employees in their Treasury departments. Sometimes the questions are ordinary—the status of a check, a request for a copy of their statement, or confirmation of the receipt of a file. But often they ask tough questions about foreign wires or lockbox issues in which I have had no training or implementation issues where there are no staff to call for answers.

Examples:

D.S. from P.W.C. sends an email listing multiple lockbox accounts where checks sent to one lockbox have been erroneously deposited into another. He also wants to know what boxes are open and which aren't, and what boxes go to what accounts, and which ones get electronic payments, and which get paper checks, and why are they being charged fees for paper checks when a certain box should only be getting electronic payments. I haven't had even one day of Lockbox training. There is no manual or reference guide. I have to call the Lockbox department for guidance about opening an investigation, and sometimes I get told this is not an investigative issue but a customer service issue, and I'm supposed to magically know the answer and handle it. They are not going to tell me. They're too busy.

Then customer A.C. sends me three pages of his ledger with foreign wires where he thought they were being debited x amount but what they were actually debited was y amount, and what is the balance in their foreign wire account, why don't their books balance, what happened to the wires they thought were being recalled, and they need an answer today.

After I tell him I'll look into it, someone else calls me about an ACH tax payment that was rejected, and they don't know why because they're doing it the same way they always do it but this time it didn't go through and maybe it has to do with codes in certain fields or maybe it needs to be right justified with a blank space and they're right justifying it with a 0. Like I know? And where would I find out? And the customer is going to be charged penalties and what I am going to do about that, too?

Then someone else calls needing to make changes to their BAI file, and I haven't a clue what a BAI file is and there is nothing in my notes about a help desk for a BAI file. And if I'm lucky they'll start in on something like integrating their BAI files with their SAP system for EDI payments and they might as well be speaking in Greek or pig Latin for all I can understand.

Next someone calls about an issuance file they sent with certain checks voided but the voided checks are now showing up with a second issuance and they want to know why. Like I'm an IT person! Where are their IT people?

My all-time most dreaded call, though, happens on a Friday morning when someone calls to tell me that they sent their automatic payroll file in as usual on Wednesday and this morning all the employees are complaining that there's no money in their checking account and they want to know why they didn't get paid. This is usually an ACH question, and that's the department that doesn't answer their phones. I have to get up and walk over to that department, so they can ignore me in person.

I have no recourse but to open an investigation and after three days of waiting it comes back to me that Investigations doesn't handle that problem, or I sent it to the wrong team. And I have maybe fifty open cases like this where I don't know where to send it or where to find the answer.

Yes, there are help lines for some issues, but often the line is busy, or you get a person who is even newer than you or maybe has an attitude if you press for an explanation.

I have sixteen different customers of my own and I back up 100 others, and the calls never stop long enough for me to research any of this. If you try to turn to your coworkers, they are all busy on their own calls, or they blow you off saying they don't know, or they play that game of starting to answer your question and then taking another call, so they don't have to complete their answer. Consequently, you sit at your desk and stare at the computer and wonder what in the hell you are going to do and what you are going to say to the customer when they call back, and how are you going to make it through the rest of the day.

This department has an incredible turnover—surprise, surprise! No one makes it past the one year required before you can post out to another department. The exceptions were Bob Baker, whom I've known for about a year and he just got fired, and Abigail Kandinski who has had a nervous breakdown. Abigail went missing in action last week after having customer problems that left her crying with hopeless frustration. She hasn't come back, and I don't think she's going to. That leaves me just about friendless except for my boyfriend, Howdy. He's not in customer service and doesn't know much, but every now and then he finds me a contact in ACH or Lockbox that is willing to help me.

Other people seem to endure, and I guess I will also, but the negative feelings are so depressing, and I don't know how to turn them around. I will have to devise new strategies of appearing to help my customers while blowing them off, so they don't know that I don't know. But I'm not good at that.

When I was crying to Howdy about it the other night, he said he was considering other options. He said the whole banking industry is so corrupt that it's a miracle it hasn't collapsed in on itself already. Between junk bonds and shaky mortgages, we could see the whole industry go belly up tomorrow and we'd all be on the street. He's taking me to a meeting with the Band of Owls tomorrow night. He says they have a radical solution. Given my unhappiness at Mirety Bank, I'm up for anything.

My brother Greg is also a member of this group. Last year, he was talked into buying a house with a Mirety mortgage that he really couldn't afford. When he got fired from his job at the casino, it only took two months for the late payment penalties and fees to put him in debt way over his head. He agrees with everything Howdy says about the banking industry. The Owls have a plan. I want to help. Maybe they'll let me.

If ever there was a disgruntled employee, Alicia was certainly one. Who knew what she might go along with to strike back at an uncaring and exploitative corporate culture? Emily thought of

Charles Manson and his band of disillusioned young women. That certainly didn't end well. Alicia also mentioned a group called the Band of Owls, and she'd had that tattoo of an owl on her back. How had Eastlake missed such an obvious tie-in?

On a personal level, to her own very deep embarrassment, Emily realized that as a trainer she was failing miserably at preparing her trainees for their job as corporate customer service representatives. In true Mirety fashion, trainers were hired, as were managers, who had never actually done the job that they were supposed to train or manage. They were given attractive binders labeled "Manual" with lots of outlines and pie charts, but those pages never really told you how to do your job.

Emily had trained people to act as liaisons, putting a customer on hold and calling the necessary department to obtain answers to the caller's questions. If that didn't work, then the representative had to open an investigation via the appropriate software system and forward it to the department concerned—for instance, ACH, or Wire Transfers, or Lockbox. That department would either resolve the issue and copy the customer service representative with the resolution, closing out the investigation, or give the representative additional information that would enable the representative to resolve it. Obviously, established procedures weren't working. She needed to start sitting with the customer service folks and learn a lot more about their jobs. Then she would revamp her training manual.

Having finished her hot chocolate, she folded up the diary pages and put them in her purse. She walked slowly back to her office thinking about the poor woman who would never get the chance to be successful at her job.

CHAPTER ELEVEN
THE SUPERVISOR

There are people who look at ease anywhere, and then there are those who look awkward and out of place anywhere you put them. Virgil Bartholomew was one of the latter. At six feet eight, he had skin the pale yellow of moldy linen and black hair so thin that his pink scalp peeked through even in the grayest of light. He squirmed on the metal chair of the interrogation room like a parent on a child's play set. There was no position at which his frame could achieve full support. He had generous feminine hips that pudged over the sides of the chair and left him off balance no matter how he positioned himself. The two detectives observing him via the interrogation room's camera almost felt sorry for him.

When they entered the room, Virgil immediately stood up to greet them, a sign of respect he hoped they would appreciate. It also brought some relief to his derriere.

The detectives introduced themselves and sat down. Detective Smith started the tape recording and made note of the day, time, and who was in the room.

"Mr. Bartholomew," Detective Eastlake began, "we just want to ask you a few questions about Alicia Kingston. We understand you were her supervisor. Please have a seat."

"Yes," he said, carefully lowering himself back down and distributing his bulk evenly so he wouldn't slide off. "She was a lovely girl. I'm so, so sorry to hear she's been murdered. I just cannot imagine who would do such a thing."

"Did you have any problems with her?" Detective Smith asked.

"Never. She was an exemplary employee."

"I have to tell you that we have her diary," Eastlake said. "She doesn't name you specifically, but she does indicate that she was very unhappy in her job and that she never got any help when she asked for it."

"This is news to me," Virgil replied, raising his voice and lifting his head, examining where the wall met the ceiling. "Does she say what she needed help with?" he thought to add. The last word came out high and whiney.

"Procedures, mostly. She reaches out to personnel in other departments such as the ACH department or the Wire Transfer department, and they don't answer her questions or respond to her emails. She seems very depressed and upset in her diary."

Virgil shook his head. His eyes took on a surprised and questioning look. How did he miss this, he wondered?

"Would she have been afraid to approach you with her problems?" Smith asked. "Would there have been repercussions if she had?"

"No, of course not."

"Could you have helped her?" Eastlake queried.

"I would have tried. I could have referred her to someone in the ACH department or the Wire Transfer department who could help her."

"Mr. Bartholomew," Detective Smith interrupted here. "You couldn't have told her yourself what she needed to know? Or personally referred her to someone at a higher level in the appropriate department?"

"Well, no, that's not how I do things. I expect my employees to know how to handle their problems. I, personally, have never been a telephone rep."

"But you're a supervisor in that department. Shouldn't you know how to do what your employees do?" This accusation came from Eastlake.

"Well, no. Not exactly." Virgil was squirming again, and the movement nearly landed him on the floor. He ran his fingers through the little bits of hair he had. He looked at the ceiling again. His discomfort was so obvious, it was unsettling.

"I'm a little lost here," Eastlake said. "You're a supervisor but you don't know anything about what the people you supervise do?"

"You don't understand," Virgil said. "I'm supposed to *supervise* them. Not do their job for them. I'm not a trainer. We have people for that." His voice had taken on a whiney hinge. He was thinking *Why are people always annoying me with their problems?*

"I'm afraid I don't understand," Smith responded. "You had an employee in obvious distress and you had no clue? Don't you monitor her calls? Couldn't you tell her mental state from her handling of her customers?"

"Quality Control reviews phone calls. I only get a spreadsheet with the results once a month. Listen, I'm supposed to *manage* them, not *babysit* them. I'm supposed to handle schedules and monthly reviews and reports to upper management. I don't need to know customer service systems to do that."

Eastlake and Smith exchanged glances; it was clear Mr. Bartholomew preferred to know as little as possible about the day-to-day responsibilities of his employees.

"What about your customers? Could any of them have targeted Alicia? Been angry at her? Found out who she was and where she lived. Maybe followed her to the park?" Eastlake asked.

"Impossible. We provide our reps with fake names to give the customers, and any correspondence would come to either our physical address or our email server. I very much doubt it could be a customer."

"Let's move on," Smith said. "To your knowledge, was there ever an employee who had a problem with Alicia or might have wanted to harm her?"

"Absolutely not."

"From your interactions with her over time, can you think of any reason someone might want to harm her?" Eastlake asked.

"No."

"Where were you Saturday night?" This came from Smith.

"Home with my wife, watching TV."

"She can verify that?" Eastlake shot back.

"Of course."

"Thank you. We'll be in touch," Smith said.

The two detectives got up, opened the door for Virgil, and watched him lumber out.

"Not much help, was he?" Smith commented to his partner.

"Don't ever let me take a job in banking," she replied.

CHAPTER TWELVE
The Blu Crab Grill

Melinda called Friday night after Emily had enjoyed another delicious pasta and broccoli dinner with Desmond. Emily was getting used to the taste of the broccoli, and the red sauce plus the chianti masked what she considered the vegetable's sour tang. She was cleaning up the kitchen and Desmond was in the adjacent pantry pouring himself a generous serving of Wild Turkey when the phone rang. She saw his shoulders stiffen as if he were disgruntled that Emily should receive a call on his private home line. Or maybe it was just the sudden clamor of the ringing itself that jangled his nerves. He may have thought she should get a mobile telephone. Emily knew that many people were getting them, now that they were being made in a more portable size, but she could not justify the expense. Melinda didn't have one yet, Kathy didn't have one, and neither did her old friends Susan and Janet. She was sure Rick had one, and that it was only a matter of time before he insisted that every member of his staff have one also.

As he disappeared into the den, Emily picked up the phone with a "Hello?"

"I've got some info on the Band of Owls," Melinda said without introduction. "They're a group of radicals who are against predatory lending by the banks—especially high-interest credit cards and subprime mortgages—and in a broader view, they're anti multinational corporations altogether. They think American businesses should market their products overseas with hefty tariffs, which of course is contrary to NAFTA. They feel American workers aren't being paid enough, and that's because we're selling stuff too cheap to Europe and China. They claim to be for the working class, whose members are being simultaneously ripped off by high-interest rates and low wages."

"I can see their point," Emily said. "And banking employees are some of the lowest paid white-collar positions. Alicia's tattoo must mean she'd joined that group. Perhaps she was plotting with them to do something at Mirety. What do you think?"

"That leaves two possibilities for her murder," Melinda said. "Someone at the bank could have found out and wanted her stopped—although, really, all they had to do was fire her—or the Band of Owls thought she might go to the bank and tell them about their plans, so they decided to kill her."

"What about domestic violence? They say it's always more likely you'll be killed by a family member than an outsider."

"Have you found out anything about her family?"

"Yes. She didn't have any except for a brother."

"What about him? Any motive there?"

"I don't think so. He's homeless and staying with Alicia. Now that Alicia is dead, he'll be homeless again."

"Too bad. Well, I'm going to drive down next weekend and stay for a whole week."

"At a hotel or with Elvis?"

"With Elvis."

"Is it too soon? Do you dare let him see the early-morning you and dispel the magic?"

"Oh, I think the magic can survive bad breath and bed head."

"Then I say, good luck, girl. He's a keeper."

After Emily hung up, she called Kathy. She was going to question her some more about Alicia but didn't get the chance.

"Why are you at home on a Friday night?" Kathy asked. "I'm just about to leave for the Blu Crab. There's a blues band at nine." Meet me there?"

"I hadn't thought of going out, but why not? See you there in twenty."

Desmond looked pained as Emily popped her head into the den and said she was going out. She noticed he wasn't reading or looking at the TV, only staring out the window at the backyard. Then she ran upstairs, changed her clothes, and banged out the back door.

The Blu Crab Restaurant and Grill was a seafood restaurant housed in a shopping center on Elkton Road, south of Newark. When Emily arrived, in her cleanest tight jeans and softest black sweater, she found Kathy at the bar. Strikingly beautiful and friendly, Kathy was always welcomed by whomever—man or woman—was standing at the rail to be waited on or nursing a beer.

"Amigo," said Kathy. "Meet my friend Bob from Mirety Human Resources. Bob, Emily."

"Hi there. What are you drinking?" Bob asked. He was tall with blonde, going to silver, hair and aquamarine eyes. Emily dismissed his good looks as out of her league, but if he wanted to buy her a drink, she would oblige.

"Rum and Coke, with a slice of lime," she replied.

"Coming up," Bob said and signaled the barmaid.

"Guess who's here?" Kathy whispered in her ear and pointed with her beer mug across trays stacked with steaming crabs and tables filled with hungry diners.

At the jukebox in the corner stood Howdy Evans, talking in earnest to a dark-haired man. Emily thought she recognized him.

"I'll be right back," she said to Kathy and started to weave her way through the tables. When she reached Howdy, he didn't see her at first. Emily didn't say anything either. She just stared in concern at the man Howdy was talking to, who was none other than the black-haired man she'd seen in Brandywine Creek State Park.

Suddenly Howdy looked up and recognized her.

"Hi," Emily offered. "Saw you from across the room and thought I'd come over and say hello."

Howdy blushed to the roots of his red hair, and Emily had to wonder why.

"Just...just catching up with an old friend," Howdy said. "Emily, this is Wyatt Dennison."

"Hi," Emily smiled at him. "Have we met before?"

"No, I don't think so," he said, but frowned as he spoke.

"You're right, we haven't," Emily quickly corrected herself, thinking maybe it was better *not* to remind him who she was.

"How are you doing, Howdy? I'm sure this has been a difficult week for you."

"I'm doing okay. I need to call Alicia's brother, Greg, to confirm funeral arrangements."

"Well, I'll leave you alone now. I just wanted to say hello. Maybe I'll see you at work in a week or two."

At the mention of work, Wyatt turned to her with a hard stare, but said nothing. Its intensity frightened Emily just a bit. She mumbled, "Glad to have met you," and fled. Kathy and Bob were waiting for her with her rum and Coke.

"He didn't look too glad to see you," Kathy noted.

"But we are," Bob said with a wink.

As the band took the stage and rowdily burst into Jonny Lang's "Lie to Me," Emily thought the night might not be a total loss. Two more rum and Cokes later, and after a few close dances with Bob, she left him with her phone number and floated out the door.

CHAPTER THIRTEEN
DESMOND'S SURPRISE

Saturday morning, as Emily sleepily inhaled coffee, Desmond bounced into the kitchen wearing a grin.

"Your coffee is sooo good. How do you make it so delicious?" she asked. She didn't have a hangover from the night before, but her body was in no hurry to move.

"The secret is freshly ground beans. I order them straight from Columbia and grind what I need each morning. It's a free perk you get for living here."

"Well, it's much appreciated. Do you have plans for the day?"

"I was just about to ask if you felt like taking a long walk with me. I need the exercise. I try to get in two or three miles a day on the weekend."

"I'd love that. Can I suggest a location?"

"Sure."

"How about Brandywine Creek State Park? I was there last weekend and loved it. Its gently sloping hills are easy on my knees."

"Perfect. I'm ready when you are," he said, pointing to his camouflage shorts and yellow tee shirt.

"Let me grab a bowl of cereal and put on jeans. Shouldn't take me more than twenty minutes."

As she had promised, Emily was ready in nineteen minutes, dressed in faded long pants and a sweatshirt jacket.

"Shall I drive?" she suggested.

"No, let me. The truck hasn't been out in a week. I try to drive it on the weekends to keep it running."

They went into the garage where Emily saw a vintage white Ford F-150 pickup taking up half the two-car garage. Desmond's Mazda Miata took up the other half. Emily sadly noted there was no room for her car.

Riding north in the rustic pickup reminded Emily of the New Hampshire countryside. She missed the Live Free or Die state with its lonely macadam roads that wound through towering pines and bisected gleaming grass fields. She had gotten used to Swansea's feel of being a rural town amid rolling acres, with homes hidden here and there beneath the sheltering pine boughs.

When he wasn't manually shifting gears, Desmond reached over and squeezed Emily's left hand. She gave him a quizzical look. Affection was unexpected. But he kept his eyes firmly on the road.

When they got to the park, Emily suggested they walk up past where she'd found Alicia's body. As they walked, she told him about finding the body and all the attending police details. As they passed the break in the wall, Emily suggested they stop for a moment so she could point out where she and Melinda had discovered the body. She was shocked to see that the police tape had been pulled down, maybe by kids playing in the area. Even more worrisome was that standing at the fallen tree was Wyatt, the black-haired man she'd seen last weekend and again last night.

"Hey!" she called to him, thinking she might ask him if he had known Alicia. But when he turned to look at them, he only scowled, and then hurried away in the opposite direction through the briar-strewn woods.

"Let him go," Desmond said. "I want to talk to you about something."

"Okay," Emily replied, sadly noting that he'd failed to comment on her upsetting experience of finding a dead body—and a murder too. Most men, most *people*, would have at least murmured something consoling and reassuring such as what an awful experience it must have been for her or that the police were sure to find the culprit. Instead, she and Desmond continued their walk up to the Hawk Watch.

"How long have you been living at my house," Desmond asked her, then answered it himself by saying, "two or three months?"

"Yes," Emily said with hesitation, thinking he was going to suggest increasing the rent.

"We seem to get along well together, don't we?" he continued.

"Well, we both like to read, we keep pretty much the same hours, and you're a wonderful cook." She smiled when she said that last part. Emily was not known for her cooking skills. Fried steak, chicken, and pork chops were pretty much her entire repertoire.

"As I recall from high school, we were both pretty good in the kissing department," Desmond observed, and with this, he halted, grabbed her shoulders, and kissed her. It was a passionate kiss, a soul-shuddering kiss, a kiss that left her breathless.

"Not bad, heh?" he said, when he finally pulled away.

Emily was speechless. She wasn't sure what she should say. There had been the possibility of Bob just the night before. Now this.

"When we were in high school, do you remember how we talked about getting married someday? What do you think? Is that why fate brought you back into my life?" Then suddenly, in the middle of the path, with brown grass and blue sky for witnesses, he got down on one knee and said, "Emily, will you marry me?"

It had been five months since her previous boyfriend, Bud, had moved out of Emily's home; he blamed her for his daughter's death. Moving from New Hampshire to Delaware had eased the pain somewhat. Emily knew it was too soon to start another committed relationship, and much about Desmond was still a mystery to her. But, in her hesitation, some hidden adolescent terror of lifelong loneliness raised its ugly head, and she whispered, "Yes."

CHAPTER FOURTEEN

MR. WISEBURG

"Thank you for coming in this morning, Mr. Wiseburg," Detective Eastlake began. She was by herself on this Saturday morning.

"Always happy to be of assistance to law enforcement," he acknowledged. Eastlake thought he sounded like a politician, which wasn't surprising. She'd found that corporate managers often had a lot in common with political glad-handers. Neither could be trusted to tell the truth.

Her guest had taken extra care with his appearance. His straight brown hair was squeaky clean and doused with a minimum of gel to keep it combed back off his narrow forehead. His large brown eyes were clear and alert, no sign of a previous night's overindulgence. His cheeks were pale with just a tinge of pink where the razor had closely scraped off every bit of beard it could without slicing his skin.

He'd chosen the sporty look of open-collared, pale blue oxford cloth shirt, crisp khakis, and tan corduroy jacket. His loafers were so shiny they glowed gold in the dusky yellow light of the interview room. Confidence shrieked from every square inch of the thirty-eight-year-old man. The detective wondered what it was all meant to hide.

"Please state your name for the record," she began as the tape recorder whirred in the background.

"Richard Alfred Wiseburg."

"And your residence?"

"I live at 6503 South Bancroft Parkway, Wilmington, Delaware."

"Your occupation?"

"Training and Customer Service Manager for Mirety Bank Corporation."

"How long have you held this position?"

"Two years."

He sat on the uncomfortable metal chair with his back gently curved along its metal spine and didn't seem to mind its hardness or its unforgiving shape. His legs were crossed as if he were perfectly at ease under interrogation. Perhaps years in corporate America had provided him with plenty of combat experience in grueling question-and-answer marathons.

"One of the employees you managed was Alicia Kingston, a customer service representative."

"Yes."

"You are aware that she was found murdered last Sunday in Brandywine Creek State Park?"

"Yes, I read about it in the Wilmington paper."

"How well did you know the victim?"

"Not well at all. I knew her name, but I probably couldn't have picked her out in a crowd. I manage about one hundred people altogether. I only see about twenty of them on a regular basis. She has never come to my attention as either an outstanding employee or as one who needed to be reprimanded for any offenses."

"Do you recall how she was rated at her last performance review?"

"I double-checked on that in preparation for our meeting today. She got a Satisfactory rating, as opposed to Excellent or In Need of Improvement. She was encouraged to avail herself of online courses in her spare time to increase her product knowledge."

"Who is her supervisor?"

"Virgil Bartholomew."

"Have the two of you ever discussed Alicia?"

"I don't believe so. We may have at a meeting around the time of the half-yearly reviews, but I'm not sure."

"Do you have any knowledge of her activities outside of the bank?"

"No."

"I've been told you dated Alicia at one time, yet you said you didn't know her well."

Rick sat up a little straighter and squared his shoulders. His face reddened at the realization that he'd been caught in a lie.

"Just briefly. Maybe once, twice, three times at most."

"And you didn't get to know her very well during that time?" There was a tinge of sarcasm in the question.

"No. We mostly went out to eat, to the movies, stuff like that. I found her very boring, really. We didn't have much in common."

"Who broke it off?"

"I did."

"Was she upset?"

"Not really. I don't think I was her type either."

"Isn't it against bank policy to date employees, especially those who report to you?"

"This was before she was one of my customer service reps. She was still in check processing when we dated."

"And as a result of dating you, did she get the job in your department?"

"Well, I knew she needed the extra income that the promotion would provide, so yes, I made sure she got the position, but I never dated her again after that."

"Did you know she was unhappy in that job?"

"No, I didn't. As I said, her reviews were Satisfactory. Could I have a drink of water?"

"We'll be finished in just a few minutes, Mr. Wiseburg. If not, I'll find you some water. Are you familiar with a group called The Band of Owls?"

"I've heard rumors. They're antibusiness anarchists. I don't know that they have the ability to do any real harm."

"Do you know if Alicia was a member of this group?"

"No." He slumped down a little as if he were tired.

"You have an employee named Howard Evans?"

Rick uncrossed his legs at this and shifted his position on the metal chair. "Yes, he's an administrative assistant."

"Are you two friends?"

Rick squirmed again.

Eastlake had no idea where she was going with this, but she'd obviously struck a nerve. He had already lied about how well he knew Alicia. Perhaps it was an even more serious relationship with Howard.

"Well, we're friendly. We get along well."

"Do you see each other outside of work?"

Rick made a movement to stand up but didn't. He glanced at the door. "We might have met for drinks after work, but that's not uncommon among coworkers."

"Have you ever invited him to your condo?"

Rick folded his hands together in his lap and squeezed. "Maybe once or twice."

"Did Alicia accompany him?"

"No."

"They were engaged to be married, right?"

Rick picked his head up and laughed. "It'll never happen," he chortled. Then he suddenly realized why it could never happen and looked shocked at his own stupidity. "Sorry, I shouldn't have said that. She was a lovely girl. I'm sure they would have been very happy together."

"Do you have any idea what might have happened to her?"

Rick regained his composure, unclenched his hands, and looked the detective directly in the eyes as he said "No."

"Thank you. You can go."

.

CHAPTER FIFTEEN

Sex and Bathrooms

On the way home from the park, Desmond and Emily stopped and bought vodka, limes, Gouda cheese, and Stoned Wheat Thins. At home, Desmond put a Jim Brickman album on the stereo, and they had a picnic on the den floor, sipping vodka martinis and eating cheese and crackers as Brickman's magical fingers serenaded them with romantic piano compositions. Eventually they wound up with their clothes off. Emily would never repeat, even to close friends, the pleasures that filled up that long afternoon. She might hint, however, that her decision to marry Desmond seemed, at the time, to be the correct one.

In the evening, as they shared another pasta, red sauce, and broccoli meal that Desmond had prepared, he broached more practical subjects.

"Maybe you should move into my bedroom," he said.

Emily agreed.

"And when we're married, I think you still need to contribute financially to the household. I don't make a lot of money as an insurance actuary."

"Of course," Emily agreed. "But I still don't get to use the washing machine?" She was joking, sort of.

"Not yet," he said.

When bedtime came, Emily gladly snuggled up to him in his queen-sized bed. She fell asleep, only to wake up at 3 a.m. in need of the bathroom. As she slipped out of bed and tiptoed across the hardwood floor, a board creaked. Desmond was immediately awake.

"What are you doing?" he asked groggily.

"Just going to the bathroom," Emily replied.

He seemed to be asleep when she came back to bed, but the

next morning he informed her that he hadn't been able to fall back to sleep.

He was tired and cranky now that he hadn't gotten his regular eight hours. "You can't get up in the middle of the night to use the bathroom," he said. "You'll wake me up and I won't be able to go back to sleep."

"Maybe we could put a rug down on my side of the bed and that will muffle any noise I make walking across the floor."

"Do you see any rugs in this house?" he asked.

"Well, no, that's true. There aren't any rugs."

"I don't like rugs. They collect dust. If you're going to use the bathroom in the middle of the night, you can't sleep in my room."

"Oh, well, I almost always have to use the bathroom."

"Then you'll need to sleep in the guest room."

"Oh…" Emily's disappointment hung in the air—half word, half sigh.

"Don't worry," he assured her. "We'll still have indoor picnics on Saturday afternoons."

The message was that sex was both important and could be scheduled. Sleeping together, on the other hand, with its opportunities for comforting and snuggling, could be dismissed. Whatever her thoughts had been the day before, on this cool Sunday morning Emily was beginning to wonder if marrying Desmond was a horrible mistake.

CHAPTER SIXTEEN
The Viewing

Emily made pancakes for breakfast later that morning. The ritual calmed her and took her mind off her disappointing confrontation with Desmond about using the bathroom in the middle of the night. As a child, her father had made pancakes for breakfast every Sunday morning after church. Now, like her father, she melted the butter and warmed the maple syrup to keep the pancakes warm. Desmond ate only two. Emily had four.

After cleaning up the kitchen, she took the Sunday paper out to the den where Desmond had put Beethoven on the stereo. Page three of the *Wilmington Reporter* noted that there were no new leads in the death of Alicia Kingston. The Business page stated that Corponium Insurance Ltd. was in talks with Mirety Bank about a future merger. The Events page mentioned the upcoming craft fair on Saturday at Hagley Museum and Library. Emily thought that might be a good activity for her, Melinda, and Elvis—but not Desmond. She suddenly realized she didn't want to invite Desmond. But how would she get out of inviting him? She had made a terrible mistake agreeing to marry him, and now she was afraid to tell him she had changed her mind. She would appear childish and inconsiderate. What she secretly hoped was that she wouldn't need to decline his offer. Perhaps in time events would play out so that their relationship would unravel of its own accord.

Alicia's viewing was from one to four in the afternoon. The funeral home was a half hour's drive away, so Emily, dressed in a dark blue suit, found a bottle of water and a pack of crackers for a snack to eat later and left around twelve thirty.

The viewing was held in an old brick mansion converted to a funeral home at Seventh and Broom Streets in Wilmington. The floors were worn to a burnished gold, the walls painted pale green, and the white curtains fell ceiling to floor with the softness of clouds. There was an ethereal feel to the rooms, as if St. Peter might be just beyond the next door. No music played, but a low hum of voices wove in between the walls and spilled out into the hallways.

The closed silver casket sat on a white-skirted dais. Above it arced a cascade of white roses, white daisies, and blue delphinium held together with royal blue satin ribbon. A blue banner proclaimed in gold print "Loving Sister and Friend."

As Emily stood in line to greet the family, she saw many familiar faces from work that she planned to speak to later. The line moved quickly, and she soon saw why. Alicia's family consisted only of one man who appeared, from age and looks, to be her brother. He sat on a folded metal chair, with unkempt brown hair brushing the shoulders of an out-of-date black suit. A scattering of dandruff flakes dotted the baggy shoulders. His thins hands were clasped in his lap. His lips were pale. His face, paler.

When she reached him, she introduced herself and explained that she worked with Alicia. His demeanor was dazed, as well it might be, given the suddenness and manner of his sister's death.

"I'm Greg," he whispered. "Greg Kingston."

"I'm so sorry for your loss," she said. "Please convey my condolences to the rest of your family."

"Oh, there is no 'rest of the family,'" he said. "Our parents have passed, and my girlfriend dumped me. There's just me. Homeless me."

"I'm so sorry. I didn't know."

"It's your bank, your friggin' bank, that's the cause of all my trouble. Please leave and take all your coworkers with you. I never want to see anyone from Mirety Bank again."

Emily was unsure how to respond, so she chose to change the subject.

"I'll go. I'm sorry for all your pain."

She reached out to touch his arm in a gesture of comfort, but he shook it off. She decided to take what might be her only chance to speak to him about his sister.

"Can I ask you just one question?"

His thin lips contorted in a grimace of pain, but he said nothing. She spoke quickly before she lost him.

"I understand Alicia had a tattoo of an owl on her back.

Sometimes that's a symbol of wisdom or sacred knowledge. Did it have a special significance to her or was it just decoration?"

"That owl was evil," he replied, his voice rising. "It caused her death!"

He stood up now, rattling the metal chair he'd been sitting on and startling those standing near him. Then he glared at everyone and abruptly walked out of the room. It was quiet for the space of a heartbeat as all eyes followed him out, then the soft hum of conversation returned. Emily looked at the person behind her in line and shrugged her shoulders. She wasn't going to tell everyone to leave. She went to the prie-dieu at the side of the coffin, knelt, and said some prayers for Alicia's soul. She added a few for the brother as well.

When she rose, she looked around the room and found Howdy in anxious consultation with Rick and another gentleman in a far corner. She went over to join them, and they stopped talking as soon as they saw her.

"Do you know why Alicia's brother is homeless?" she asked.

"He's lying," Rick sneered. "He lived with Alicia."

"You don't like him?" Emily asked.

"I think the police should be looking at him as a suspect," Rick said.

"Her own brother?" Emily asked.

"He was a parasite, living in her home, asking her for money. Maybe he benefits from her death." Rick spoke quietly so others wouldn't hear him. Emily wondered how much was true.

"He did own a home," Howdy offered, also in a low tone. "But he was foreclosed on by the mortgage company."

"By us?"

"No, we'd sold the loan to someone else by then."

"That's what all the banks do," the third gentleman said.

"Hi, I'm Emily, a coworker." She faced him and continued, "Couldn't he afford it in the first place or did he have bad habits?"

"I'm Sean, a reporter." He didn't offer his hand, only ran his fingers upwards through his disheveled Afro and frowned at her. "I've been investigating these bad mortgages. He shouldn't have gotten the loan in the first place."

"Alicia couldn't talk him out of it. He kept saying if the bank thought he could afford it, then he guessed he could," Howdy explained.

"But he couldn't?" Emily wanted to pursue it.

"Well, that's a subject for debate," Rick broke in. "Let's get out of here, Howdy." Rick put his hand on Howdy's elbow to hasten their departure. "I need a drink. See you tomorrow, Emily."

The reporter walked away in a different direction. Emily was herself about to leave when Kathy came up behind her and grabbed her arm.

"Someone you have to meet," she whispered in her ear.

Emily allowed herself to be led across the room to where a very tall man with black hair was lounging against the wall. His appearance was awkward, too young for the stomach that draped unattractively over his belt, and too old for the smooth skin of his face.

Kathy announced, "Here is our Auntie Vie, short for Virgil Bartholomew. He knows everything about everyone. You'll want to stay on his good side. Auntie, this is the new trainer, Emily Menotti."

"Shall I call you 'Auntie Vie' also?" Emily asked as she shook his proffered hand. It was a large, soft paw, reminding her of a sheepdog.

"Please, except in front of management. It doesn't sound very professional. I'm one of the customer service supervisors."

"Were you Alicia's supervisor?"

"Afraid so. I knew there was trouble in paradise, but I didn't anticipate murder."

"Any thoughts on who would have wanted to kill her?"

"My, we do get right to the point, don't we?" Auntie Vie laughed and put his right hand on his hip. "None that I care to publish at the moment."

"Stick around Vie and you'll be the first to know," Kathy suggested to Emily. "He's on the ground floor of all the office scuttlebutt."

"'Butt' being the operative word," Vie said, then laughed at his joke. "How long have you been in banking, Emily?"

"Maybe fifteen years here and there."

"Then you know it's all gay men and bitchy women."

Emily was shocked to hear the rumor stated so bluntly, and she disagreed with his assessment. She doubted the suits in the corporate offices in Manhattan were either gay or women. She figured Vie was not a person to make an enemy of, however, so she chose not to challenge him. She did opt for making an exit. Auntie

Vie's brand of gossip made her uncomfortable.

"Gotta fly," she said. "Good to meet you, Auntie Vie. I'm sure I'll see you on the floor. And, Kathy, I'll see you tomorrow. Take care all."

She was glad to escape and take a moment on the walk to her car to think about Auntie Vie. There was a nasty tone to his comments. Would he have had a motive to kill Alicia?

As she was about to unlock her car, she saw Greg sitting on the curb next to an aging VW microbus. His head was in his hands, and his shoulders were shaking. Emily guessed he was crying. She walked over to him and sat down on the curb next to him.

"It's all too much, isn't it?" she said. "I'm so sorry about your sister. I guess I should tell you that I was one of the persons who found her."

Greg picked his head up and brushed at his tears with his suit sleeve. "You? The police said two old ladies on a hike."

"Well, yes, that would be me and my friend Melinda."

"Did you see anything else? Did you see *anybody* else?"

"No, I'm afraid not. She was under a pile of leaves. We happened to see her foot sticking out. We uncovered her and checked for a pulse. That's how I knew about the tattoo. I'm so sorry. There was nothing we could do." She thought it best not to mention Wyatt since she didn't know if he had a connection to the murder.

"Thank you for telling me. I guess I should go back in, but I don't want to. I'm so angry at the bank because they foreclosed on my home. I can't stand to see anyone who works for them."

"Can you stay at your sister's until the end of the month?"

"I can, but then I *will* be homeless. Oh well, I have some friends who might take me in."

"I understand that it wasn't Mirety who foreclosed. That they'd sold your loan to another bank."

"You don't get it, do you?" he said, tears gone and anger returning. "Would you like to see what they did, not only to me but others like me? Would you like to see the result of their promises? I could show you. It's only a few minutes away. I'm not going back in. Are you?"

"No, would you like me to drive?" Emily had her doubts about the reliability of the old minibus.

"Yes, please."

CHAPTER SEVENTEEN

PARADISE FORECLOSED

Greg directed Emily south of Wilmington to a community located off Route 405. The entrance had a weather-beaten wood sign with art deco green lettering proclaiming the community to be PARADISE FOUND. The dirt and scrub grass comprising the surrounding hundred square yards looked anything but celestial.

The macadam road they followed was torn and rutted, scars left by numerous construction vehicles many months, maybe years, before. The scene was a landscape of abandoned homes, each built in a rectangular, shoe-box style with aluminum siding and vinyl trim. A few had an aging Saturn sedan in the driveway or a rusting minivan, but most displayed empty driveways. The sunbaked homes looked neglected and weather-damaged, with grass lawns turned to weeds and bleak treeless vistas. A poverty version of Monopoly where the money had long ago run out and the players had left for other pursuits.

Greg asked Emily to stop at 517 Angelic Lane, where he pointed out an aqua-blue version of the elongated-box theme with black shutters and trim now showing gray gashes where the paint had peeled. A few window screens were torn, and unopened mail littered the walkway to the front door.

"Home sweet home," said Greg, "for all of thirteen months."

"What happened?" she asked.

"They cut back my hours, and I fell behind on my mortgage payments. Once you miss a payment, they start adding fees and penalties. Even if you manage to scrape together the missing mortgage payment, you're still hundreds of dollars in the hole, and there's no catching up. Each month it's more fees and more penalties. When they let me go three months later, I just gave up and moved out."

"I'm so sorry. I guess the mortgage companies aren't very sympathetic."

"Just try finding out who your mortgage company is! By the time you're making your second payment, you've got a letter in the mail saying the mortgage has been bought by ABC Bank and now you should send your payment there. Two months later, you get a letter saying it's now been sold to DEF Bank and there's a new payment address. If you have a question and you call the DEF Bank 800 number, you're told ABC is still handling it. So, you call ABC who says no, DEF should be handling it, and of course, you're on hold for fifteen or twenty minutes each time." Greg was now pulling at his hair and shaking his head back and forth. "It makes you crazy! And no one cares, really. No one friggin' cares!

"Push one for English," he continued, voice rising. "Two for Spanish. Welcome to the main menu. How can I help you? Push one to hear your balance, push two to make a payment, push three for current mortgage rates, push four to hear the time and weather, push five to stay on hold until your ear falls off, and push zero to be placed on hold for twenty minutes while our system transfers your call to the next available customer service representative who won't be able to answer your question…aagghh!!!"

Greg was bouncing up and down in his seat now, rocking the car as it crawled along the empty service roads of the community. To the casual observer, he and Emily must have looked like refugees from a Cheech and Chong movie in which addled druggies were experiencing bad acid trips. In Greg's case, maybe not too far from the truth.

Emily put her hand on his arm to calm him down. Like every other person who used the telephone to contact a business these days, she knew the frustration of automated answering systems.

"I know what you mean," she said. "It's enough to drive any sane person bonkers. But let's get back to how you lost your home. I saw a show on *Sixty Minutes* about subprime mortgage lenders. Is that what you had—a subprime mortgage?"

"Yes, I did, which I guess was my own fault. I should have paid more attention in math class. I didn't understand about amortization and interest rates, etcetera, etcetera."

"And who does?" Emily sympathized. "They don't teach that kind of practical stuff in school. At least they didn't in my high school. It's all about teaching to test scores."

"I talked to my neighbors, who, as you can see, have mostly moved out. They didn't understand either. All they knew was that some hot-shot realtor told them that they could afford a house four times their income. Four times! Do you know how they justified that?"

"Not really. Doesn't seem right to me."

"Here's what they told us. If you borrowed say $80,000 at 9 percent for 30 years, you'd have a monthly payment of $644."

"Nine percent! That seems high."

"Yes, but subprime interest is higher because the borrowers are higher risk. The plan, supposedly, is to get the marginal people into the housing market so they can start to build equity. Then, when they've made their payments on time for a few years, built up their credit, and paid down $5000 on the principal, they can refinance $75,000 on a regular mortgage at 8 percent interest and have a payment of only $550 a month, saving $94 per month. Or at least that's how it's supposed to work.

"But it doesn't. What people don't understand, and I didn't either until it happened to me and I started doing the research, is that most of us subprime people are already having problems making ends meet. If you lose your job and don't find another one right away, or the wife gets pregnant, or you have a car accident and you can't work, or need an expensive a car repair, bam! You need extra money and the mortgage doesn't get paid. Then you're behind and fees and penalties kick in, and before you know it, you feel like it's hopeless, so like me, you just walk away."

"Seems to me such a practice shouldn't be legal," Emily offered, wanting to be sympathetic.

"It's perfectly legal. Problem is what's legal isn't always moral," Greg replied. "A lot of people are not smart enough to make that distinction. If it's legal, they think it must be all right."

"Unfortunately, that's true," Emily agreed. She thought about the casinos in Atlantic City. When she had lived in Delaware in the eighties, she knew husbands who had routinely gambled away the next month's mortgage payment and left wives and children collecting food stamps to survive. What the public schools needed to teach were critical thinking and decision making.

Suddenly quiet, Greg gestured to the silent community they were surveying. The empty houses looked to Emily like tombstones now, monuments to dashed hopes and broken dreams.

"How many people still live here, do you know?"

"I'd say sixty percent are abandoned. The other forty percent are just hanging on because they don't want to lose their investment."

"What a sad place to live," Emily said.

"Not as sad as living in your car," Greg answered back.

"Are the banks to blame," Emily asked, "or the people who thought they could afford these homes but really couldn't?"

"I guess it's a perfect storm of unregulated bank greed, a depressed real estate market that doesn't provide a living for all the agents who have invested in it as a career, and the folks they take advantage of who just weren't born with the smarts to do the math. I fell victim to it. I'm not proud of it. I dared to dream the American dream of home ownership, and I lost. End of story."

"From what I've seen, I've got to lay most of the blame on the bankers," Emily said. "They have created an atmosphere where the loan officers are encouraged to make risky loans to people they know will default, and then, they bundle those mortgages up and sell them off to mitigate the risks. It's a travesty to con people into buying something they can't afford. Think of the heartache and misery they've caused."

"Well, I'm doing something about those bastards."

"What can you possibly do? These decisions are out of our hands."

"I can't tell you," Greg said. "Just watch the news. You'll see."

"You're not going to break the law are you, Greg? Nothing illegal?"

"Nothing for you to worry about. Me and my friends are just going to stir up a little trouble. Didn't you do that back in the sixties to protest the Vietnam war?"

"Well yes, but what I did was all peaceful. Sit-ins and candlelit marches and signing petitions. Nothing violent. I wasn't a member of the SDS."

"Don't worry. It'll be okay. Better take me back now. I'm feeling calmer, and I need to speak to the funeral director about tomorrow."

"Thanks for showing this to me," Emily said. She started the car and headed back into Wilmington.

After dropping Greg off at the funeral home, she headed back to Odessa. She wondered if she should start looking at apartments since it was looking unlikely that she and Desmond would marry. Home ownership might not be the best choice in the current real estate market.

CHAPTER EIGHTEEN

O'FRIEL'S

On Monday, instead of attending the funeral for Alicia, Emily took Detective Eastlake's advice and visited the Division of Motor Vehicles to update her driver's license. She chose to use the city office, a tiny brick building just off Bancroft Parkway, because it was usually less crowded than the office on Airport Road.

After showing her New Hampshire license, two bills verifying her new address at Desmond's home in Odessa, and her title document, she received a Delaware registration certificate for her car. Then she took an eye test administered by a sleepy matron, which involved staring into a viewer and identifying orange, pink, and green numbers to verify that she wasn't color-blind. Next, she was directed to a hallway where a Cindy Lauper wannabe with pink hair and black boots snapped her picture and then pointed her in the direction of some molded plastic chairs and told her to wait. Much to her surprise, she found a familiar face among the smattering of strangers.

"Heh, Bob, ditching work today too, I see."

"I figured everyone would think I was at Alicia's funeral, so instead, I'm getting some personal errands done. This place is mobbed on the weekends." He seemed at ease in his bank uniform of navy suit and dark tie, although Emily thought she preferred the gray cotton jersey and black jeans he had worn Saturday night.

"Did you know Alicia well?" Emily asked.

"I knew of her. I can't tell you more than that. Professional confidentiality."

"I understand." She hesitated to offer that she had found Alicia's body.

"How do you feel about the merger with Corponium? The bigger, the better? Or does it jeopardize your job?"

"I try not to worry about those things. I've been through four or five mergers in my thirty-five-year career as a Human Resources manager. Twice I've been riffed. How 'bout yourself?"

"I've had a long and bumpy career. I originally worked for Chase Manhattan here in Wilmington back in the eighties. Then my husband, who's now my ex, was transferred to New Hampshire, where I got a job with Swansea Savings Bank. In January of this year, they were bought by Metro Bank, who then shut down my department and offered me a job in their offices here in Wilmington. I no sooner moved here, though, then we merged with Mirety, so who knows what happens now. Banking is just crazy. I enjoy being a trainer, so I'm going to stick it out and hope for the best."

"Robert Bowie!" came a voice over the loudspeakers. "Please go to Counter One."

Bob quickly retrieved his license. He returned to the seat next to Emily.

"When you get your license, let's go someplace for a cup of coffee before we go back to work. I'm guessing no one will be in the office until noon."

Just then, "Emily Menotti..." squawked over the speakers, and she made the same trip to the pickup counter. When she returned, Bob was standing and waiting for her.

"Where to?" he asked.

"Let's go to O'Friel's. They should be open by now."

"Ah, you're thinking Irish coffee?"

"No, not for me. But feel free. I just love the pub atmosphere. I'm sure that in a previous life I lived in England or Ireland and spent all my free time in one."

"It's close to work too. I'll meet you there in ten."

They parked their cars in the bank garage and walked the short distance to O'Friel's. Bob's assigned spot was on a different level than Emily's, and he was quicker to arrive. She spotted him waiting for her in a dark mahogany booth in a corner. She didn't see anyone from her department, so she breathed a sigh of relief and sat down.

Within a few minutes, her mood changed. She wasn't sure if it was because she should have been at work, or her concern for the trustworthiness of Bob, but she felt uneasy here in the dusky shadows of the Irish pub. They both ordered black coffee and were silent for a moment.

"I think this was a bad idea," she finally said. "I'm not sure why, but I don't feel right being here when I should be at the office."

"You were alright going to the DMV," Bob pointed out.

"Yes, but that was a task that needed to be done. This is just goofing off."

"Maybe it's something else. Maybe it's the ghost of Anne Marie."

At his words, a chill snaked through Emily, and she involuntarily glanced around, as if expecting to catch a glimpse of the pale young face and stunning brunette tresses of one of Wilmington's most famous murder victims.

"Did you know her?" Emily asked.

"No, I never met her. But I spoke to her once on the phone when I wanted to schedule a meeting with Governor Carper."

"Well, if she was going to haunt some place, this might be it. The O'Friel's were her friends." Emily glanced around again. Goosebumps broke out on her lower arms as the bartender propped open the front door and the resulting breeze stirred the curtains.

For a moment, she thought she saw movement in the mirror behind the bar—a quick half-face turning away. She was startled and jerked upright, and then understood that, in that sudden movement, she was only seeing her own light brown hair stirred by the doorway's breeze. Or was it?

Anne Marie Sinead Fahey, like Alicia Kingston, had been murdered. She was only thirty at the time of her death in June 1996, shot by her married lover when she tried to break off their affair. She had a wide, expressive face, a sprinkling of freckles, and sad dark eyes. Emily had been living in New Hampshire when she died, but her friends in Delaware had kept her apprised of the hunt for her killer, his capture, and his subsequent trial and conviction. It was a landmark case in that a guilty verdict had been returned without Anne Marie's body ever being found.

Anne Marie had rented rooms only one block from where the Brandywine River flowed under the Washington Street Bridge. She'd been shot in her lover's home near Rockford Park, within a short walk of the river. In a flash of gunpowder, she became just one more lost soul wandering its banks, thrust by tragedy into the afterlife with no time for preparation. Emily shivered again and wished she'd brought a sweater. The breeze from the door, left open for the fresh air, felt more like an exhalation from the grave.

The waitress brought their coffees. Emily stirred two pink sugars and a dollop of cream in hers; Bob sipped his black.

"Are you a native?" she asked him.

"No, 'fraid not. I moved here from Pennsylvania about five years ago when I was divorced and got the job with Metro, right before Anne Marie's murder. Any other famous crimes I should know about?"

"Can't think of any. We're pretty low-key. Oh, one other factoid, we're the incorporation capital of the United States. More than half of all the Fortune 500 companies are incorporated here. And there's no state income tax on Delaware corporations."

"Maybe you should be a tax lawyer," Bob kidded.

"No thank you! I'm just well versed in my state history. At the university, we have to take a whole semester's course on little old Delaware. And I'm sure you know why all the banks moved here."

"Yes, no usury laws. Banks in Delaware can charge any amount of credit card interest they want to."

"That's us. If you didn't get blown up in the duPont powder mills in the nineteenth century, or chemically poisoned in the twentieth, the banks will financially ruin you in the twenty-first."

"My understanding is that banking was supposed to be an eco-friendly industry. I've read about all the pollution problems Delaware has had with the oil refineries in Marcus Hook and Delaware City. Unfortunately, the blue-collar jobs pay much better than the white-collar jobs."

"And pink-collar jobs pay even less. I'd better get back. Ready?"

Bob graciously paid their bill and they left, walking back to the bank in companionable silence. As Emily exited the elevator on the tenth floor, Bob called out, "Lunch sometime?"

"Sure," Emily called back, thinking she didn't have time to explain about Desmond and her tentative engagement. Well, they could talk about it if Bob ever did ask her out to lunch.

When Emily got back to her desk, there was a brief note saying "See me." She recognized Rick's handwriting. What now?

CHAPTER NINETEEN

In the Lion's Den

Rick had scored a corner office as manager of Customer Service and Training. The glass walls faced northwest onto Delaware Avenue, and his chair was angled so that his back was to the view of Interstate 95 slicing north to south through downtown Wilmington between Jackson and Adams Streets. The construction had demolished a strip of neighborhood a block wide and ten blocks long. Its location had forever divided the bonds of a close and vibrant African American community for which the city fathers were never forgiven.

Emily had been in high school in the sixties as the concrete supports were erected and steel beams lowered into place. She walked within its shadow each day to and from school along Van Buren Street and over the Brandywine River. From the vantage point of her journey down Monkey Hill, past Josephine Gardens, and across the bridge, the interstate looming high in the firmament above her looked less like a roadway and more like a skyway to heaven. Thirty-five years later, it was just one more dirty, concrete highway overcrowded with aging cars and tractor trailers.

"What did you want?" she asked Rick, concerned that he had noticed her absence both at work and at the funeral.

"Have a seat," he smiled with his politician's grin. Emily considered it was really bad news if he wanted her to sit down.

"It's come to my attention that things are not going well in Customer Service. There's a lot of complaints that our representatives aren't resolving issues as quickly as they should be. I think training should address it."

"Okay" was all Emily said. She wasn't sure where this was going.

"I realize you're new here, so I'm not suggesting that any of this is your fault, although I'm afraid upper management sees it that way."

Oh no, I'm being fired, Emily immediately thought.

"However, I've talked them into giving you a second chance."

Sneaky bastard, she thought. *He threw me under the bus and now he's pretending to rescue me.*

"I've noticed that you don't have any training classes in progress now, right?"

"Yes."

"I'd like you to begin sitting with the subject matter experts, meaning the most proficient representatives in certain areas of expertise, starting next week. I've talked to some of the supervisors, and they are going to provide me with a schedule of who you'll sit with on which days. Will that be a problem?"

"No. What's the time span for this project?"

"About a month, and then you'll have another month to rewrite the manual. I'll want a progress report from you every Friday morning, copied to Kathy, Howdy, and the customer service supervisors. Any questions?"

"Not right now."

"Okay. Talk to you later."

Emily rose from her seat and started to leave, but then, Rick called her back.

"Emily, remember for the future, I saved your ass."

"Yes, sir."

She had never called him "sir" before, but somehow it felt appropriate now, like a private acknowledging his drill sergeant who held all the reins of power.

CHAPTER TWENTY

THE BAND OF OWLS

Greg parked on a side street off West Main Street in Newark. There were three or four fraternity houses in the area, so beat-up vehicles were not uncommon. His derelict VW microbus would feel right at home.

He didn't smoke often, but he felt like smoking now, so he lit a Salem Light while he double-checked his recording device. He was sure that someone from the Owls had killed his sister, but he needed proof. Perhaps someone at the meeting tonight would say something incriminating.

He had joined the Owls to strike a blow at corporate America, especially the banks—those bastards who had put such a stranglehold on the economic opportunities of the new century. Like the catch twenty-two of being unable to get a job without job experience, you couldn't get credit without a credit history, and then when you did get credit, one missed payment and your credit was ruined. They pushed credit cards on naive students, charged enormous interest rates, and forced those in dire circumstances into bankruptcy. The Owls believed that if they could disrupt the banks enough, hack in and wipe out payment record memory, they could free millions of people from their crushing debt and damaging credit histories. And what would it harm the banks? Their presidents and CEOs made millions, even billions. A little loss would barely touch them.

He had invited his sister to join, but something had gone wrong there. They were suspicious of her contacts at the bank. They thought she might have warned management of their plans. He knew she hadn't. In fact, she had spoken to him gleefully of seeing Mirety go down in the symbolic flames of computer file annihilation. The Owls, however, were a hypersuspicious bunch, so the question still nagged at him—did they kill her to silence her?

He ran his fingers through his greasy hair and double-checked that his jeans jacket completely hid the tape recorder that was stuffed in the inside pocket. He finished off the last swallow of a half-pint of Popov vodka and threw the bottle to join four or five other empties on the microbus floor, along with McDonald's wrappers and empty soda cups. At the end of the month when the rent on Alicia's apartment would be due again, he would have to move permanently into his VW, unless he could come up with a scheme to make some money.

Unable to think of any reason to delay his task, he pushed the Start button on the recorder, exited the microbus, and made his way up to West Main Street, where he crossed over the two-lane blacktop to the white two-story house where the meeting should have already begun. He stood on the porch and gave the secret knock—two raps, a pause, three raps, a pause, then two more raps—and waited for the door to open. A face briefly appeared at one of the heavily draped windows; then the door was opened just wide enough to let him in. It was hastily shut behind him.

"Heh, brother," whispered the curly-haired conspirator of androgynous mien. "You're late."

"Not feeling well" was all he said and shouldered his way through the twenty or so young men and women to a spot near the fireplace. They were an unhealthy-looking bunch: long-haired, unkempt, reeking of marijuana and body odor. They wore mostly dark clothes and disgruntled expressions.

Wyatt Dennison leaned on the wall between the two front windows, which were covered with dark quilts to keep light out and conversation in. He was gazing at the tall man with Rasta hair who was speaking. Greg didn't know this man's real name, but he was known in the group as Kaboom. He'd gotten that name because he was always urging the group to blow up buildings. Luckily no one took him seriously. The group leaders, as much as they despised corporate America, didn't want to see a repeat of the Sterling Hall bombing in August 1970 when a University of Wisconsin-Madison physics researcher was killed, and three others injured, at a time when the building was thought to be empty.

"I trust my brothers and sisters are all keeping to our pledge to buy only products made here by union workers in the U. S. of A."

"Yeah!" came enthusiastic voices from the scattering of members lounging on sofas and chairs in the semidark room.

"Thank you. First on the agenda, we have a demonstration set for downtown Wilmington on Saturday, November eleventh, Veterans Day. The chicks are making posters. Am I right, Tara?"

"We're ready," shouted a purple-haired girl sitting on a sofa.

"Second on the agenda, our gamers are looking at some nasty ways to disrupt Mirety Bank's computer systems, which they've asked me not to share with anyone just yet. My contacts assure me they can get our guys access when their plan is ready to go. We're thinking the Christmas holidays are a good time to create havoc. Lots of folks coming and going, lots of parties, people on vacation, people slipping out to do shopping, nobody paying close attention to who's coming in and out. We'll cover all this in more detail at future meetings. Any questions?"

No one spoke up. There were murmurs and head nods, but no raised voices. Greg figured most were too stoned to come up with any coherent projections.

"Meeting dismissed," Kaboom said.

As people began to leave, Greg sat down next to Tara, the purple-haired girl.

"Sorry about your sister," she said, raising purple eyelids and parting purple lips.

"Who did it, Tara?" Greg asked.

"I wouldn't tell you even if I knew," she said, then she shakily got to her feet and walked away.

Wyatt sat down next to him.

"How's things?" he asked Greg.

"I'm surviving."

"You need to know I was keeping an eye on your sister, but I didn't see her the night she was killed. I do know that Howdy was going to tell her that we didn't want her in the Owls. I didn't trust her. I thought she might rat us out."

"Why?"

"She's so bourgeois, man. Like another Patty Hearst. It was a frigging game to her. She wanted to marry Howdy and live in a little rose-covered cottage. She would've ratted us out in a heartbeat to save her ass."

"Do you think Howdy killed her?"

"I don't know, man. I don't think so. I mean, why? He loved her."

"You haven't spoken to the police?"

"Hell no. Why? I can't have the police snooping around me, around us. I'm very sorry about your sister. She was a sweet girl. But the revolution takes precedence. You understand? You were screwed over by the banks yourself."

"Yeah, I know. Why are you waiting so long to move on this hacking job? Too much time. Someone might let something slip between now and Christmas."

"Not to worry. Kaboom planted that thought to see if it surfaced somewhere outside the group. Someone's got loose lips. We've made plans to strike a lot sooner. You'll see. By the way, any luck finding a job?"

"No. But I've got a lead on a cable job with a subcontractor for Comcast. I should hear next week."

"Good luck, bro. Gotta fly." Wyatt stood up and went upstairs.

Greg was feeling tired, angry, and thirsty. He wondered if he could score a soda from the fridge. He pulled himself up from the couch and headed to the kitchen through a dining room with no table, only old wooden chairs and a scattering of tray tables, half of which held computers and copy machines barely discernible in the gloom.

He rounded the corner into the half-light of the ancient kitchen still blemished with fifties style aluminum cabinets and countertops of stained Formica. Lounging on an aluminum step stool sipping a beer, still dressed in business suit and tie, was Rick Wiseburg.

"What the hell are you doing here?" Greg asked. "Does Wyatt know you're here?"

"Of course! He invited me," Rick smiled.

"But you're the bank," Greg sputtered. "You'll warn them of the Owls' plans."

"Now why would I do that?" Rick stood up and pretended to dust dirt off his suit. "What difference does it make to me if the bank's computer systems fail? Maybe I'm just the person to guide them through a restructuring of their security systems."

"God, you're something else," Greg said, shaking his head. He restarted his walk to the fridge at the other end of the room, jerked open the door, and took out a Pepsi.

"Heh, don't be upset, man. I've been thinking. The foreclosure on your home isn't final yet, is it?"

"No, not yet. But I don't have any electric or water, so I can't live there."

"Maybe I could pull some strings. Talk to the folks in Mortgages. If you could find a job, maybe I could help you work something out."

Greg sipped his soda and thought about this. Rick was not to be trusted. His sister had told him this many times. But what did he have to lose at this point?

"I might have a job with a Comcast subcontractor. So, yeah, look into it."

"I'll be in touch," Rick said and tossed his empty beer can in the sink. "See ya 'round," he said and left.

Greg didn't respond. Then he remembered that the tape recorder was still running. He smiled to himself; reopened the fridge and took two more Pepsis, which he stuffed into his pockets; and left.

Back at the car, he turned off the tape, removed the cassette, and locked it in the glove box. He figured you never knew when it might come in handy.

CHAPTER TWENTY-ONE
Customer Service Research

Tuesday morning, remembering Alicia's anguished diary entry, Emily decided to tackle the problem Alicia had had with directing calls and inquiries to the ACH department. Like her, Emily chose the scenario of employees not finding their paychecks in their checking accounts to be a matter of utmost importance. Emily thought that if she had to field that call, she'd want to be able to resolve the issue as quickly as possible.

She asked Kathy, the other trainer, who she would call in the ACH department, and Kathy gave her the names of the shift coordinators: a woman who handled the seven to three shift and a man who handled the three to eleven shift. Emily called the woman, and it went straight to voicemail. She left a message and busied herself with answering email and planning other areas of research. Having not had a callback in an hour, she dialed the number again. Again it went to voicemail, and again she left a message.

Emily found other work to keep her busy for another half hour, but she still had no call from the woman in ACH. Tired of waiting, she decided to visit the department, which was only one floor up. When she got off the elevator, she asked for directions to the ACH department and found the woman, whom she identified by her desk nameplate, talking to a coworker who was sitting on a low filing cabinet.

"Hi," Emily said to her. "I'm Emily. I'm one of the Customer Service trainers. I've been trying to reach you. Did you get my phone message?"

"I've been too busy to get my messages," she replied with a frown. "Can't you see you've interrupted a meeting?"

"I'm sorry. I was hoping I could schedule a time to get together with you to talk about procedures."

"I'm too busy. I have too much work to do. Please don't bother me with your training problems," she said, rolling her eyes in obvious annoyance and returning her attention to the other woman sitting on the filing cabinet.

"Could I send you an email with some questions?" Emily asked, not wanting to give up.

"You can try. I can't promise I'll have time to answer it," the woman replied. The other woman glared at Emily as if daring her to say something else.

Defeated, Emily turned and left. She understood Alicia's frustration. She hated going to Rick for help. Perhaps she'd stop back at three and speak to the gentleman on the evening shift.

When she returned to her department, she saw Kathy and told her what had happened.

"I don't understand," Kathy replied. "She's always such a sweetheart to me. And she's so funny. You should hear her stories about her kids."

"I guess it's just me," Emily said.

"Try again at three. He's a lot friendlier. Too friendly, actually. I avoid him 'cause he's always asking me out."

"Now who do I talk to about Lockbox?"

"That's an easy one. I have some cheat sheets at my desk. I gave this information to Alicia, but maybe she lost the papers."

Emily followed Kathy to her desk, and after much drawer banging and file rifling, Kathy handed her five pages of charts dividing lockbox numbers into ones that accepted wires, one that accepted checks, which had fees, which didn't, and the appropriate contact numbers and email addresses for questions and investigations.

"Have you ever called these numbers?" Emily asked. "Are they up-to-date?"

"No one's complained."

"Well, I'm going to check these out."

"Good luck. Will you let me know if they're wrong and give me the right ones?"

"Of course."

Emily spent the rest of the morning and part of the afternoon calling and revising Kathy's list. Most of the numbers were correct, but contact names had changed, as had email addresses and fees. She spent a good part of the afternoon creating a new spreadsheet and condensing all the information into one handy cheat sheet she could distribute to new hires.

At three thirty, she was back on the elevator and up to the ACH department to meet the evening shift coordinator. She'd decided not to waste her time calling.

She found him rushing from a wire mesh IN bin next to the daytime coordinator's desk to his own desk, and then back again as workers on the floor kept coming up to it with correspondence and written requests.

"Hi, I'm Emily…" she began, but she didn't get far.

"I know, I know," he said, interrupting, "and I'd be glad to help you but now is a bad time. As you can see, all the people whose work didn't get done this morning are expecting me to do it now before they go home."

"Oh, I'm sorry."

He stood still for a minute and gave her a slow once-over. He was ten years her junior and handsome in a Slavic, gray-eyed way that Emily found attractive, although with the age difference she was sure he wouldn't feel that way about her.

"Look," he said and scribbled something on a piece of paper. "Here's my email address. Send me your questions, and I'll answer them later tonight when things calm down."

"Thank you," she said and retreated back the way she had come. She hoped he was telling the truth. She probably wouldn't have the nerve to come back.

Before she went home, Emily called Detective Eastlake to find out if the police were any further along in their investigation. She was surprised when the detective picked up on the first ring. Her voice, however, sounded rushed and impatient.

"Eastlake" came the growl into Emily's ear.

"It's Emily Menotti. I was calling to ask if you've had any luck finding out who killed Alicia Kingston."

"We've got a few folks under investigation. Unfortunately, that now includes you."

"Me? I didn't even know her!"

"So you say, but you work for the same company, you're in the same department, you train people to do her job, you report to the same boss, and now you're hanging out with her brother. You never mentioned, when you were speaking to me, that you were familiar with the Band of Owls. Why did you withhold that?"

"I didn't think it was relevant," Emily lied. She hadn't chosen to share for precisely the reason Eastlake was now giving her a tough time. She didn't want to be part of a police investigation.

She decided to try and change the subject. "I wanted you to know that I've read Alicia's diary and she seemed very unhappy at her job and very critical of management at the bank. She talks about Howdy and Greg being members of the Band of Owls. Have you investigated *them*?"

"We're investigating all the members, and that includes you."

"What? I don't know anything about the Band of Owls."

"Then how come you're on their membership list?"

CHAPTER TWENTY-TWO
A MESSAGE

Emily nearly dropped the phone. Who would have put her name on the list? Was someone trying to frame her? This was crazy.

"What!?! No, I'm not a member. Who would put my name on their list? I didn't even know Alicia and would have absolutely no motive to harm her. Who put my name forward as a possible suspect?"

"I can't tell you that, and I'm not hauling you in for questioning right now, but as I said before, don't leave town."

"And you have no other leads? No other evidence, no DNA or fingerprints or correspondence pointing to someone else?"

"Nothing that I can share with you."

"Okay. I guess I'll wait to hear from you."

"And you will be." With this, Eastlake disconnected.

Emily drove home on autopilot, barely noticing the five o'clock traffic on Interstate 95 going South and, later, on Routes 13 and 9. She changed into jeans and sweatshirt as Desmond made pasta, red sauce, and broccoli. They spoke little during dinner, Desmond mostly complaining that management was piling on the work and he was determined not to give them any overtime. Emily was too preoccupied with her own thoughts to do little more than murmur, "I see, that must be hard," or something similar while she mulled over in her mind who would have given her name to the police and, more importantly, who would have added her name to the membership list of the Owls.

She offered to clean up dinner to make up for her lack of communication. Desmond grabbed a bottle of Wild Turkey and a tall glass of ice, kissed her forehead, disappeared into the den, and closed the door. "Don't disturb me" were his parting words. Not "Good night" or "See you in the morning."

When she'd finished with the dishes, she glanced through a crack in the door and saw that he sat with the lights out and the stereo turned up, listening to Beethoven's Eroica. She knew him well enough now to know that he would drink himself into a stupor and then stumble to bed at one or two o'clock in the morning.

When she thought about his behavior, the secretiveness, the darkened room, the music, it had all the earmarks of a forbidden romance or an affair. In this case, the other woman was Lady Alcohol.

On Wednesday, Bob called and asked her to have lunch with him. He was now on her list of possible suspects, not for any good reason, but simply because she didn't know him that well and had suddenly made himself friendly. Was he a clandestine member of the Owls? Could he have known Alicia better than he was willing to admit? Could he have even killed her?

"O'Friel's okay?" he asked. "Can you do eleven forty-five? We'll beat the noontime rush."

"Perfect, see you then."

At eleven-forty Emily left her desk, walked to the elevators, and quickly found an empty one to take her to the ground floor. Two minutes later she was pushing open the heavy door to O'Friel's, finding it particularly balky. As she put her shoulder into it, she felt an unseen mass of woman's hair brush across her face, long strands with that sweet scent of just-shampooed locks. It lasted barely a second, but it startled her, and the door fell back and almost knocked her over.

"Whoa, are you okay?" Bob asked as he came up behind her and caught the door in its backward swing.

"I think so," Emily said. "Heavier than I thought it was."

They entered and noticed there were very few people dining; they had beaten the noontime rush. The bartender came around from the bar with two menus and motioned them to a booth. As they began to fold themselves into the seats, Emily looked at the silverware displayed on the tabletop. Usually, each set of knife and fork was neatly rolled up in a napkin, but here the napkins had been put aside, and the forks and knives were scattered across the tabletop. Perhaps it was only her imagination that had been kicked into overdrive by the aura of scented hair at the door, but it looked to Emily like the silverware had been arranged to create the letter "E" or "W." Who or what had done that?

A waiter noticed and mumbled, "What the hell?" Then he quickly scooped them all up. "I'll get you new silverware and napkins," he said. "I don't know how that happened."

Emily thought she did know, and the "W" stood for Wyatt. Was someone or something trying to tell her that Wyatt had killed Alicia? But she couldn't think of what the motive would be.

"You look like you've seen a ghost," Bob said as they settled into their seats and the waiter brought glasses of water and new place settings.

"This is a spooky place," Emily commented. She tossed her head a bit to shake off the vibe of otherworldliness that she'd just encountered, then smiled, "I'm famished."

She ordered the O'Friel's Chef Salad, and Bob got a burger with fries. Both added Diet Cokes.

"So how has your day been?" Bob asked.

"Not bad. I'm trying to research ACH procedures for my next training class, but I'm finding that the people who do the job are too busy to talk to me. I have to figure out a way around that."

"Just keep pestering them. That's what I do. Make yourself annoying enough, and they'll realize that if they just talk to you, then you'll go away."

"Do you do that with people who are in senior positions to yourself?"

"Are these people in senior positions to you?"

"No."

"Then don't worry about it. However, people in senior positions you treat differently. If they won't help you, you have to find someone else who will. I've learned the hard way not to make a nuisance of myself. It'll come back to haunt you at review time."

"Ah yes, the dreaded review. I remember when I first started working that I was surprised at how the women were always much tougher on me than the men. So much for sisterhood."

"Women see you as a threat. Men never do."

"Ouch! I never thought of that."

"You learn a lot in Human Resources. Oh good, here's our lunch. Now I'm relieved of revealing any more of our secrets."

"I'll work on you some more another time," she promised him as she picked up knife and fork to neatly slice the hardboiled egg in her salad.

"I hope you do," Bob replied, took a bite of his burger and

chewed it quickly. "I wanted to tell you to watch TV tonight," he said after he swallowed. "There's a spot on the local eleven o'clock news about Mirety and a few other banks. It has to do with their mortgages and the housing development Paradise Found. You might find it interesting. It seems there's been a lot of complaints about predatory lending and Mirety's name has come up."

"I'll try to stay up," Emily replied, taking another bite of salad. "I have trouble staying awake after ten, but I'll make the effort. Any official comment from the representative in Human Resources?"

"No, it's not my area of expertise. We'll talk about it later. Say, what are you doing this Saturday? There's an arts and crafts fair at Hagley Museum. Would you like to go with me?"

"My friend Melinda will be visiting from New Hampshire this weekend," Emily explained as she cut into rolled up slices of turkey, ham, and cheese. "She'll be staying with her boyfriend in North Wilmington. I don't know what their plans are, but they usually include me. Would you want to make it a foursome if they're interested?"

Emily thought briefly of Desmond. Here she was newly engaged and accepting a date with Bob. She would have to find a way to speak to Desmond and call off the wedding plans. Clearly, her heart was not in it.

"I'd like to meet your friends."

"I have to warn you. Melinda has a bit of ESP. Sometimes she senses the presence of spirits, the spirits of people who have died."

"Hagley is where the duPont powder mills were. There will be lots of spirits I should think...unless they've moved on. I don't know much about these things."

"But you won't make fun of her?"

"Never. I've an open mind when it comes to the paranormal. Will it make her unhappy or uncomfortable?"

"We can let her decide. Is that okay?"

"Fine. We could always go somewhere else, like Longwood Gardens—although that's right down the road from the Brandywine Battlefield Park. She'll have a tough time escaping the dead in the tristate area."

"She's from New England, where the ghosts of the revolution wander with the witches and harass the spirits of the religious zealots who put them to death. I think she'll be okay."

When Emily dragged herself home from work that evening, tired and discouraged by the difficulties she was encountering putting together the new training material for the customer service reps, she found Desmond in a chipper mood and deftly rinsing off two pounds of uncooked chicken wings.

"Will you fix these in the oven for us?" he asked. "I love your recipe."

Oven-baked chicken wings was one of the three or four dinner recipes at which Emily excelled. Since she was going to be blowing him off on Saturday, it seemed like a good idea to butter him up tonight.

"Sure, just let me change."

In ten minutes she was back in the kitchen, dunking the wings in eggs and bread crumbs, then arranging them on aluminum foil-covered cookie sheets. The trick to making the wings a low-fat treat was to spray the aluminum foil with nonfat cooking spray first, then the wings themselves before putting them in the oven to bake for thirty-five minutes. Once the wings were in the oven, she got herself a beer from the fridge and joined Desmond on the back porch.

She took a deep breath and enjoyed the lingering summer-like temperature while her eyes feasted on the orange, red, and gold of the swamp maples that lined the far property line of Desmond's home. Her allergies would make her stuffy in the morning, but she didn't care. The beauty of the season was worth it. She imagined a lifetime of sitting on this porch, beer in hand, enjoying each season as it rolled past. This brought her mind back to her relationship with Desmond. His beautiful home was a strong pull, but not enough on which to build a marriage.

Feeling sorry to lose the mood, she said to him, "Melinda is coming down to stay with Elvis this weekend. I might go with them to the arts and craft fair at Hagley. Do you mind?"

She held her breath, waiting for him to ask if he could come too. What would she say?

"I'm so glad you have plans." His response surprised her. "I'll be tied up all afternoon. Someone from work is having a birthday luncheon at a restaurant in town—I forget which one; must ask him tomorrow. Anyway, it's just work people, no spouses, no dates. I imagine I'll be gone three hours or more."

"Oh." Her feelings were hurt at the exclusion, but more

importantly, it sounded like a lie. She'd been in the workforce for almost thirty years, and she'd never come across a coworker weekend get-together when dates and spouses weren't included. Was Desmond likewise having second thoughts? She hoped so. It would make the eventual breakup a lot easier. However, right now it played to her advantage.

"Well, that works out perfect," she said.

Then the phone rang.

"It's probably for you," Desmond complained. "You get it."

Emily got up and went into the kitchen.

"Hello?"

"Stay away from Bob Bowie," growled a deep male voice.

"Who is this?"

"A friend. Bob's not what you think he is."

"If you really care what happens to me, tell me who you are."

"Can't," the voice grunted and hung up.

Damnation, she thought. *I was just starting to trust him.*

CHAPTER TWENTY-THREE

QUESTIONS

After dinner, Emily offered to do the cleaning up. She took her time rinsing all the dishes before putting them in the dishwasher, scrubbing all the countertops, and sweeping up the floor. It was nine o'clock by the time she dried her hands and hung up the kitchen towel on the oven door. Desmond was already in his den—lights out, Beethoven on the stereo—well into his tryst with Lady Alcohol.

Emily opened another beer and called Melinda. She told her about Bob and his suggestion that they attend the Hagley Arts and Crafts Fair.

"Sounds like fun. Elvis hasn't mentioned any plans to me, although he might have some. I'm leaving tomorrow morning to drive down. I'll call you tomorrow night after I've spoken to him. Anything else going on?"

"Desmond asked me to marry him."

"He what? Really? And you said?"

"Yes."

"Are you sure?"

"No. Not at all. I think I've made a mistake."

"Tell me about it."

"I've just been so lonely, Mel. I miss Bud. I miss you. I miss New Hampshire. Des takes such good care of me. He cooks, he does my laundry. He cleans. He likes to read. He's intelligent and thoughtful. He has a beautiful home. He's employed. What more could I ask for?"

"Do you need taking care of?"

"Of course not, but it's nice for a change."

"It always comes with a price."

"I know. But, Mel, he's terrific in bed—my god, he makes me

happy." Emily paused here. She was uncomfortable talking about sex. "It's hard to walk away from that. But...he can be very odd. He worries me."

"How is he odd?"

"I'm not allowed to use the washer and dryer because I might break them. In his defense, they are very old. And after he washes my clothes, he folds them and puts them in my drawers, which means he can go through my things."

"You know that isn't good."

"I know. But the worst thing is that we can't sleep in the same bed together at night because if I get up to use the bathroom it wakes him up and he can't get back to sleep. It means I have to sleep in the guest room. No cuddling under the covers."

"Well, I know a lot of couples where one of them snores and the other sleeps in the guest room."

"I suggested that we put down a rug so the floorboards wouldn't creak, but he doesn't allow rugs in his house. Are you getting the picture?"

"I'm afraid so. He's a control freak. I'm not saying that's a deal breaker. But is that how you want to live your life?"

"That's just it, Mel. I don't think so. I thought I might be in love with him, but I'm not. And he drinks—a lot. He shuts himself away almost every night and gets drunk." Emily sighed.

"So now I've met Bob and—while I have to put him on my list of suspects in Alicia's murder because he works at the bank— mostly I enjoy his company, and I want to see him again. If I were in love with Des, don't you think it wouldn't even occur to me to see someone else? Geez Louise, here I am, fifty years old, shouldn't I have figured this out by now?" Emily laughed and gulped some beer. "What idiots we old ladies are. Don't we ever learn? You seem to have got it right with Elvis, though."

"Knock on wood when you say that."

"So, you'll call me tomorrow night and we'll talk about Saturday?"

"For sure."

She went into the upstairs sitting room and turned on the TV. Luckily the quiz show *Who Wants to Be a Millionaire* was on from nine to ten. Trying to guess the answers, Emily got about half. It kept her awake until ten, and then the *48 Hours* magazine show kept her interest until eleven. At ten-fifty there was a brief spot highlighting the upcoming news. It showed the reporter Emily had met at Alicia's viewing, the Afro-coiffed Sean, interviewing a homeowner at Paradise Found.

"What do you want the world to know, Mrs. Washington?" Sean asked a young woman with a toddler on her hip.

"We was robbed and those bankers should go to jail," she spat out and backed it up with an angry glare and outward thrust of her chin.

"More at eleven" came the voice-over.

At eleven, Emily sat through the usual Philadelphia area news: a fight in Germantown, a fire in Kensington, a drug bust in Strawberry Mansion. Could there be a more incongruous name for a neighborhood, Emily wondered, than Strawberry Mansion in Philadelphia? Her mind wandered. Back in the nineteenth century, farmers had sold strawberries and cream to the public from a former judge's home near Fairmont Park. It was still maintained as a historic property. She often wondered if small children, upon hearing its name on the news, thought it was the original home of their doll Strawberry Shortcake. Her attention snapped back to the TV. The announcer had moved on to the lead story, and there was Sean introducing his latest installment of his investigation of bank fraud and predatory lending.

The screen was filled with previously filmed footage of the abandoned and foreclosed-upon properties of Paradise Found. The camera panned to an old sign Sean had found that was put up before ground had been broken on the first lot. "Paradise Found" it read, and underneath "Financed by Metro Bank"—the bank that had been bought earlier in the year by Mirety. The camera panned to the bottom line of the sign: "If you've got a paycheck, you've got a home."

"This is the come-on that attracted so many unsuspecting, hardworking people who thought that they could finally afford a home of their own," Sean could be heard saying. "What did they tell you, Toni?"

The woman with the toddler spoke: "That with only my pay stub and a down payment of one thousand dollars, I could buy a three-bedroom home for my family."

"Did they tell you how much the home would cost?"

"Not exactly. They just told me that the mortgage would be one thousand dollars a month and that I could afford it."

"Were they telling you the truth?"

"Well, yes and no. The mortgage was one thousand dollars a month, but I didn't know that didn't include taxes and insurance. When those were added in, it was fourteen hundred dollars a month, and that was more than I could afford."

"But you bought the home anyway?"

"Well, I didn't find this out until settlement day, and by then I thought it was too late to change my mind. Besides, we were all so excited about the house."

"And then what happened?"

"After three months of making my payments on time, the baby got sick, and I didn't have enough money to buy medicine and make the mortgage payment."

"What did you do?"

"I called the mortgage company, Metro Bank."

"What did they say?"

"They said they couldn't help me because they'd already sold the loan to another bank. I forget the name, but they gave me the phone number."

"Did you call them?"

"Yes, I did, and they said to just pay whatever I could afford. They didn't tell me about the interest and penalties that would accrue on the unpaid portion."

"And then what happened?"

"I started getting these bigger and bigger bills for hundreds of dollars over what I had expected to owe."

"What did you do?"

"I called the mortgage company again. But they told me my loan had been sold again, and that I should call someone else. I called the new bank, and they said they didn't have the loan. I called back the old bank, and they put me on hold for forty-five minutes until I finally hung up."

"What is the situation now?"

"My home is being foreclosed on, but the banks are so mixed up about who owns what that no one has actually shown up yet to put me out of my house."

"What will you do when that happens?"

"Go live with my mother, I guess."

"How much money have you lost?"

"Probably fifteen thousand dollars altogether, and they say

I owe thousands more. I don't understand it. Why did they tell me the home would only cost me one thousand dollars a month when it actually cost me fourteen hundred? They're liars and cheats. They've ruined my life and cost me money I could have put down on another house. They should go to jail."

"Thank you, Toni. This is Sean Olvedo. More tomorrow when we'll tell you how Metro and Mirety Banks have responded to our requests for information."

Emily turned off the TV and prepared for bed. She felt sorry for all the working-class families whose lack of knowledge had allowed them to be taken advantage of by unethical bankers and realtors. She wished she had the magic answer to teaching teenagers and young adults the banking facts of life.

Emily found it hard to fall asleep that night. When she stopped worrying about the victims of predatory lending, she thought about Bob. She hadn't mentioned the warning phone call to Melinda. No sense worrying her while she was four hundred miles away in New Hampshire.

How could Bob be dangerous? She thoughtfully reviewed the facts she had so far: a young woman found strangled in Brandywine Creek State Park with a tattoo of an owl on her back; too few police leads; the girl's diary that stated her unhappiness at the bank; her soon-to-be homeless brother accusing the bank of having something to do with her death; the bank's duplicity in predatory lending tactics; and, finally, Alicia's writing that Howdy was taking her to a meeting of the Band of Owls, a group who offered a possible solution to the bank's misdeeds.

Emily had to admit that she had not put tough questions about the murder to other bank personnel. The only person she had discussed Alicia's death with was Alicia's brother. A brother would fit the first police category of family member as most likely suspect. And where did Bob fit into any of these scenarios? The only thing suspicious was his sudden appearance in her life and his interest in being with her. Maybe she was being played, but why? It was so depressing to think that and to know that she just couldn't relax and enjoy being with him. She'd have to be on her guard.

Emily fell asleep thinking she had been slacking off and needed to get busy questioning more people at the bank about Alicia. Then she'd see if that prompted any more phone calls.

CHAPTER TWENTY-FOUR

CUSTOMER SERVICE

Thursday morning, still waiting for Rick's list of customer service reps to sit with, Emily decided to get a jump start on the project by visiting a customer service supervisor. She didn't see Rick in his office, so she sent him an email to let him know where she'd be for the new few hours. Then she took the elevator to the Customer Service floor and found Virgil Bartholomew's desk.

"Hi," she said, feeling too awkward to call him Auntie Vie. He looked at her and grinned. "What's up, buttercup?" he asked.

"Rick asked me to do some research for a new training manual. Is it alright if I sit with one of the representatives and listen to their calls? Because I've never done this job, it'll be very helpful in my training."

"I should say," he agreed. "Why don't you sit with Karen Osgood. She's been here a year. Sad to say, that makes her an old-timer."

"Thanks," Emily said. "Anything else I should know?"

"Oh, there's lots you should know, but I'm not the one to tell you," he said with half a leer and then looked back at his computer screen. "Oh, she sits right next to Alicia's desk," he added as Emily sighed and walked away.

Emily found the desk easily and grabbed Alicia's chair. Pulling it over to Karen's cube she smiled and said, "I have Virgil's permission to sit with you for a while and listen to your calls. Do you mind? We're updating the training manual, and I want to make sure that our procedures are correct and relevant."

"No problem. Auntie Vie let me know you were coming. Oops. Here's a call."

Since there were no extra headsets, Emily couldn't hear what the caller was saying, but she could follow as Karen made notes and then accessed various screens to find the customer's account information. They only needed a copy of their most recent statement, and that was easy enough to send out. This was something Emily knew how to do.

"Do you have any problems with ACH calls?" Emily asked her, remembering all the difficulties Alicia seemed to have.

"Luckily few of my client calls involve ACH issues. When they do, I usually email the guy on the evening shift. He seems a bit more sympathetic to me than the daytime person."

"Did you know Alicia well?"

"Not well, but we were work buddies. I know she was struggling with the job. I tried to help her when I could, but it seemed that the days when she would have the most difficulties were the days when we were the busiest. They track our time on the phone and the times we're available. I couldn't refuse a call when I was trying to help her. She found that very frustrating. I don't think she had the aptitude for this type of work. Excuse me, here's another call."

Emily sat silently as she spoke to someone who was calling for an update on an issue Karen had opened an investigation for earlier in the week. She explained that she hadn't heard back from the Overseas Wire Research department but that she would contact them when she got off the phone and call the customer back that afternoon.

"What was it about Alicia that made you think she couldn't do this job? What do you think that I, as a trainer, should be on the lookout for?" Emily asked Karen.

"She was such a romantic. And such a perfectionist. That almost sounds silly to put those two characteristics together, but I guess you could say she was a perfect romantic." She smiled sadly at this. "She wanted everything to be beautiful and right and just, and she had no patience with waiting for it to happen. If she couldn't be the best customer service rep possible right away, then she didn't want to do it. Excuse me, another call."

I thought about this as Karen handled her call, this one a bit more difficult as she had to pull up multiple screens and review old emails before she could tell the customer that the issue had been resolved and the money put back in their account.

"I've met a lot of people like that. I'm surprised she didn't post out to another job."

"She probably would have eventually. Some days I thought she might even quit right then and there, but I used to cajole her into staying. She loved to watch the Olympic ice skaters on television and often expressed admiration for the women who would attempt a difficult triple axel, say, only to fall on their butts in front of the whole world, and then get up and finish their program with grace and enthusiasm. I used to say to her, 'Alicia, remember the ice skaters when they fell. They always got up and kept going. Be an ice skater, Alicia. Pick yourself up and keep going.'"

"And it worked?"

"Most of the time. Oops, another call."

Emily got up from her seat and walked around the cubicle wall to where the photo of Alicia and Howdy still sat on Alicia's desk. She was laughing in the photo. The two smiling faces glowed golden with her hair and their love and their future. But her soft brown eyes held a glint of sadness at the corners.

Emily went back to her seat and waited for Karen to finish with her call.

"Did she ever talk about problems with Howdy or her brother or her boss?"

"All three, I'm afraid. Howdy would break dates and forget to call. If you ask me, he was getting cold feet about the engagement, but I was afraid to tell her that. Then there was her brother who was freeloading in her apartment. She was upset that he hadn't found a job yet. And then there was Auntie Vie who was none too happy with her job performance. Said she was ruining the stats for Customer Service. He may seem a little swishy at times, but he's plenty ambitious."

"Oh, I have no problem with anyone's sexual preference," Emily responded. "I'm open-minded on this issue."

"Don't let him fool you. He's as straight as you or I. He's got a wife and four children. There may even be grandchildren. I think it's just a front to pick up on office gossip."

"Poor Alicia. She doesn't seem to have been tough enough to deal with this environment."

"I can only agree."

It was ten o'clock now, and the calls were coming in one after the other. It was clear that Karen wasn't going to have any more free time to talk. Emily stayed for another hour and made copious notes, extrapolating what she could from Karen's conversation and the screens she could see on the computer. Then she thanked Karen for her time, replaced the chair at Alicia's desk, and returned to her floor.

That night Emily had a dream. It was late at night, and she was walking up Talley Road to Weldin Pond where she used to ice skate as a child. The streetlights illuminated her path as she crunched across the snow-covered field where she saw ahead of her a young woman already skating on the pond. The skater was gliding around the edges, then slowly shortening the circles, making them smaller and smaller, until she was approaching the center of the pond. As Emily drew closer, she could hear music in her head. It was Beethoven's Moonlight Sonata, and the hypnotic lower register notes were matching the scrape, scrape, scrape of the lone skater's blades on the ice. Dah-da-da, dah-da-da, dah-da-da—the ghostly figure with fine-spun golden hair and dressed in a long dark coat skated round and round and round.

As the sonata became louder and darker in Emily's head, the figure reached the center of the ice and began to twirl. At first her arms were held above her head in a ballerina pose, and then, as she slowly lowered them, she went into a sitting spin with one leg bent beneath her and the other stretched in front of her. Emily stood openmouthed in awe, watching from the shore, as the skater spun faster and faster in a spray of ice and mist. Suddenly, a wind sprung up, howling and gusting, pelting Emily with ice, forcing her to close her eyes, and finally pushing her down into the snow. She struggled against the stinging pellets, bucked the wind with her head and shoulders, and forced herself to sit up.

She opened her eyes, and when she did, the wind stopped. All was quiet. There was no wind, no music, and no spinning skater.

The howling of that wind, however, echoed in Emily's ears and would not quiet until she woke herself up and looked at the clock. Three o'clock. Dead time—when the spirits roam the earth.

CHAPTER TWENTY-FIVE
Not Exactly TGIF

On Friday morning Emily knew she needed to speak to Howdy to learn more about his relationship with Alicia, Alicia's ties to the Band of Owls, and more about Alicia herself. He had been out of work on compassionate leave, but she hoped he would come in today, if only briefly, to catch up on email. She didn't have his phone number and it wasn't on the department's list of numbers for emergencies."

Howdy wasn't at his desk when she first arrived, so she spent most of her morning reviewing the email response she'd received from the evening shift coordinator in ACH. He'd been very helpful, supplying her with charts, timelines, and tips for the customer service representatives. Emily now needed to incorporate his information into the format of her training manual.

Around eleven, she got up from her desk and headed for the break room for a third cup of coffee. She noticed that the air in the office felt different today. There was a faintly acrid scent in the air, sour and industrial. She thought that perhaps there was work being done in the building requiring blow torches or metal drilling. It was unpleasant and upsetting.

Passing Howdy's desk, she found him there, scrolling through email and making notes on a legal pad. She stopped and smiled at him.

"How are you doing?" she asked.

He turned to her, and she was shocked to see his ravaged face. There were black bruises under his eyes from lack of sleep, and his cheeks were pale and hollow. His hair was combed but greasy and stuck together in that unwashed way hair gets after a few days, matted down like sea grass after a hurricane. His eyes were dull and only partially focused on her, as if some other stupendous event was in the forefront of his thoughts. He said, "Huh?"

"You don't need to be here," she said gently and touched his arm with her hand. She decided now was not the best time to question him. "Go home and get some rest."

He shook himself and brushed her hand away.

"I have a meeting with Rick. Now." He jumped up, and Emily noticed his white shirt and khaki slacks were wrinkled as if they'd been slept in, maybe repeatedly. "I've got to go."

Her eyes followed him as he stumbled down the aisle between the cubicles and then turned in the direction of Rick's office.

I hope Rick sends him home, she thought. *He's a mess.*

Emily looked up to see, of all people, Auntie Vie standing in the aisle in front of her.

"Our boy's in bad shape," Auntie pronounced from his six-foot-eight height. "Now I wonder why that could be. And why does this place smell like someone's been shooting off a cap pistol?" Then he turned and walked away.

Emily looked after him in astonishment. What had he been doing there? Then she heard a noise that startled her out of her thoughts. At first, she could have sworn it was the hooting of an owl—but how had one gotten into the building? Then she realized it was a scream, and it was coming from Rick's office. Kathy and Nora came running. They found Howdy kneeling on the floor, pummeling his chest with his fists, and shrieking in pain.

Rick was kneeling next to him and had his arms around his shoulders, but he wasn't strong enough to stop Howdy from trying to hurt himself.

"Call an ambulance," Rick shouted, and Nora went to the desk and called Security. She managed to get out her message in between Howdy's soul-piercing wails of distress. When she replaced the receiver, she said that Security would call the ambulance and bring the EMTs upstairs.

The three women stood helplessly scattered about the office, struggling with both pity and horror as Howdy's screams subsided while Rick crooned to him, "It'll be all right, you'll see, we'll make this right." He whispered this over and over again, like a mother with her frightened child. The women stood there silently, willing Howdy to get ahold of himself and wishing there were something else they could do, but of course, there was nothing. As they watched in silent agony, Norah put her arm around Kathy's waist to comfort her and, then, included Emily as she joined them.

It was a forever of pain and discomfort before the EMTs arrived; Howdy continued to moan and shudder in anguish. When the EMTs did arrive, they gently removed Rick's grasp and took Howdy's vitals. Howdy slumped to the floor. The EMTs raised him up and gave him a shot of something to stop his trembling. All watched in silent grief as the EMTs lifted Howdy, strapped him to a portable chair, and took him out to the hall and into an elevator.

No one said a word. No one knew what to say. After a moment Rick announced, "I'm going home. I don't give a damn what the rest of you do." He grabbed his coat and marched out of his office.

Emily went back to her desk and sat down. Kathy came and sat on her filing cabinet.

"I've never seen anyone do that," Emily said. "I would have thought he'd reconciled himself to Alicia's loss by now. What terrible grief! I wonder if Rick said something to him to set him off?"

"Maybe Rick said something unkind about Alicia."

"Have you heard any rumors this week about her from people on the floor?"

"I've heard Alicia was slacking off and in danger of being fired. She used to be a good employee, but recently she was coming in late and not following up on her investigations. People were saying she was just distracted with the wedding preparations. But she was also overheard to say some pretty disparaging things about the bank, things you shouldn't be saying on the floor where it might get back to management."

"Did anyone warn her?"

"I don't know. I only heard she'd been talking about her brother losing his house, and other people losing theirs, like it was a conspiracy. That kind of talk can get you in trouble."

"Well, she certainly pissed someone off. Poor Howdy. Let's hope he's just had a temporary setback."

"I agree."

Later that afternoon, Emily got a call from Rick.

"Just checking to see if you needed me for anything," he said. "I probably won't be coming back in this afternoon."

"Have you heard anything about Howdy?"

"He's doing better. They have him at the Wilmington Hospital under sedation. He can't have visitors. They'll probably move him eventually to some place like MeadowWood or the Rockford Center for more specialized psychological care."

"Then he's had a real breakdown?"

"I don't know. Maybe not. We'll see what the doctors say.

I might stop in to work tomorrow to make up for the time I've missed today. Will you be in?"

"No. I'm going to the Hagley craft fair. Poor Howdy. I guess Alicia's death has just been too much for him. And, Rick, I know that Alicia and Howdy were involved with a group called the Band of Owls. I don't know if that had anything to do with her murder. Do you know how involved they were with them?"

"Why are you asking me about that?"

"I was just curious. You and Howdy are such good friends, and Howdy was engaged to Alicia."

"I wouldn't know anything about any terrorist organizations. If you're smart, you won't poke your nose into them either. I've got to go. You know how to reach me."

He hung up quickly, leaving Emily surprised and bewildered. Rick had called the Band of Owls a terrorist organization. She hadn't offered that. Howdy, Alicia, and her brother were members. Who would a terrorist organization target? Rick himself had said multinational banks. Alicia worked for one such bank. Perhaps she'd let something slip and they'd killed her to silence her. The police had this information, but they weren't going to give any of it to Emily because they thought she was a member too.

She needed to talk to Greg. Where would she find him? Alicia's apartment? She could ask Gina where it was. The end of the month hadn't arrived yet. Maybe he was still living there.

At Mortgages on the first floor, Emily walked back to Gina's office only to find her desk not only unattended but empty. Her nameplate was gone, photos of her family were gone, not even a pen or paper clip had been left lying on the smooth desktop. Emily went back out to the receptionist's desk.

"Does Gina have a new office?" she asked.

"Fired," the woman said. "Yesterday. That's all I know."

"And her boss?" Emily asked out of sheer curiosity.

"Promoted to the head office in New York. We're closing the Mortgage department in Wilmington. I'm just here to help the movers."

"And all the people who've applied for mortgages recently?"

"Who cares?" she said and went back to her crossword puzzle.

Stymied, Emily thought of another tactic. She went to Karen in Customer Service.

"I need to contact Alicia's brother, Greg. You don't by any chance know how I could find him?"

"Well, he's probably still living in her apartment. I could give you the phone number."

"That would be wonderful."

Taking the number back to her desk, she called and was glad to hear Greg answer on the first ring.

"Hi, Greg. This is Emily Menotti. Remember me from the viewing? We drove out to your housing development together. I thought I'd give you a call and ask if you've found out anything more about your sister's murder. I haven't had much luck."

"I have been doing some investigating," he said. "but I can't tell you anything just yet. I want to get more proof. Then I'll let you know."

"What are you going to do?"

"I haven't figured that out yet."

"Please be careful."

"I will."

Emily hung up the phone and glanced up to see someone just exiting the aisle of cubicles. Had he been listening to her call? She jumped up and ran to the end of the aisle in time to see Auntie Vie entering the hallway where the elevators were located. Had he been spying on her? Kathy had painted him a harmless busybody. Emily had to wonder just how harmless he really was.

CHAPTER TWENTY-SIX

HAGLEY MUSEUM

When Melinda called Emily on Friday night, Desmond was already ensconced in his den with his drink and his music, far gone into an alcoholic stupor.

"Why don't you come to Elvis's home tomorrow?" Melinda offered, "And then we can all go to Hagley in one car. I'd love for you to see his house."

"Great idea. How about you give me the directions, and I'll call Bob so he can meet us there also. Is that okay?"

She couldn't ask Bob to drive to Desmond's to pick her up. Meeting him at Elvis's home was the only solution. She also wanted to check out the residence of the man who'd captured her best friend's heart. In New Hampshire, Emily had fallen for a handsome, articulate man who turned out to live in a pigsty of hoarder proportions. The romance had ended when she walked in his front door. She hoped Elvis's home was normal.

Melinda gave her directions, and they planned to meet at eleven the next morning. When Emily called Bob, he suggested they meet at Hagley; he had some errands to do first. They'd connect at the entrance at eleven thirty.

Saturday morning, Emily headed up Interstate 95 to Route 202 and, from there, made a quick turn onto Foulk Road. After a quarter mile, she veered right onto Wilson Road, then made a right turn onto Shipley Road, proceeding down the smooth two-lane blacktop with old brick homes and stately, mature trees to a wooded area known as Bringhurst Woods. Elvis's home sat in a cleared space on the edge of the woods. It was a modest stone edifice dating back at least a hundred years with sharply angled dormers and an acutely pitched black roof that pierced the sky with narrow points above each window. The lower half was shaded by an expansive porch roof supported by stone pillars. This porch roof had been modernized with skylights angled to allow the sun into the house. Four front windows were framed with soft white curtains. Brilliant red geraniums, still thriving in the October sun, filled planters on either side of the walkway. Elvis had done everything he could to alleviate the exterior gloom of the forbidding stone façade.

Emily had just parked her car and started up the walk, when out of the front door burst Melinda who, glowing with happiness, proceeded to skip up the front walk to meet her friend. They hugged, Emily noting that Melinda had dyed her hair a slightly more golden shade of red this time and that it was more becoming than before, although her sparkling eyes and joyous spirit spoke volumes of beauty in themselves.

Elvis appeared at the doorway, cropped white hair combed up straight like a rock star. He smiled at the women and extended his hand to Emily.

"Welcome to my home," he said. "Come in. Did you have any problems finding it?"

"No. I've just realized I've seen your house before. Did it used to belong to your parents?"

"It did. I grew up here and moved back in when my father passed five years ago."

"Did you know my friend Faith Woolhats, or her younger sister Christine, in high school? I think Christine had a crush on you. You were in her chemistry class, and she'd talk about you all the time. We'd all get in my car and she'd ask me to drive by here, hoping to catch a glimpse of you. Christine was sad you never succumbed to her charms."

"Didn't I? I probably never knew how she felt. I don't remember any girls having a crush on me in high school. I was kind of shy."

"It's so amazing to see you again," Emily continued. "It's such a trip to run into people from the past and marvel at the careers and families they've acquired. I hope it's mostly been good experiences and not too many tragedies for you."

"Can't complain," Elvis replied. "We're just about ready to go. Shall I drive?" He wanted to change the subject; this was not the time or place to reminisce.

"Please do," Melinda said. "Emily and I have to talk. Is Bob coming?"

"He'll meet us at Hagley," Emily explained.

While Melinda collected her things, Emily peeked into the living room where a gleaming bust on a pedestal in one corner of the room commanded her attention.

"That's Pallas," Elvis explained, noting her interest. "Look around in there and see if the décor reminds you of anything."

At first, Emily thought the room appeared a bit gloomy with lattice work on the upper half of the windows, and shutters on the lower half that would have blocked the light completely if pulled across. There was a stone fireplace flanked by bookshelves and on the wall opposite the windows, a wide desk flanked by twin *Gone with the Wind* lamps in pink glass with a white floral design. Beneath the windows was a more modern sofa with purple velvet cushions. Something flickered in the back of Emily's brain, but she didn't make all the connections until she turned to look back at Elvis standing in the hallway and saw the item attached on the ledge over the door.

As she looked up at the black bird perched as if to swoop down upon her, Elvis said, "Nevermore."

"I love 'The Raven,'" Emily cried out. "You must be a fan of Edgar Allan Poe.

"He's creepy, isn't he?" Melinda said, and Emily paused for a moment, not sure if she was referring to Elvis or Poe.

"Both," laughed Melinda, second-guessing her. "Let's go."

They climbed into Elvis's RAV4 and drove to Foulk Road where they swung over to Route 141 and shortly, thereafter, arrived at Hagley Museum. All the while, Melinda brought Emily up-to-date on the happenings among their friends in New Hampshire.

When they arrived at Hagley, they parked under a tree and were glad to see Bob just parking his own Volvo only a few cars down the row. Introductions were made, everyone shook hands, and they began to wander past booths of handicraft goods. Everything was on display—from glassware to pottery to woven blankets and crocheted hats. There were framed artworks of all media, especially oil and watercolors. Emily would have loved to purchase a stained-glass window, but realized she had no place to hang it. Around noontime, their appetites were aroused as they passed booths of aromatic homemade bread, cakes, pies, and cookies. There were even two stands for honey collected from local hives. Emily purchased a jar to spread on toast.

They walked across the grounds to the Belin House Organic

Café where they bought personal pizzas and lemonade. Since it
was a beautiful day, they opted to eat outside on the porch. On the
way to Hagley, Emily and Melinda had discussed telling Bob about
their finding of Alicia's body at Brandywine Creek State Park. As
everyone was enjoying their pizza, Emily took a deep breath and
began the story.

When she finished, Bob said, "How awful. I've never seen a
dead body outside of my parents' in hospice and at a funeral home.
You must have been shocked and saddened. Horrified maybe.
Have you had nightmares?"

"No, thank goodness. But I think about her all the time and see
her lying there, so alone." Emily turned to Melinda.

"What about you? Any bad dreams or recurring thoughts?"

"I've had a few bad dreams, but no communications. Sorry.
Nothing to help us find out who killed her."

"Bob," Emily turned to him. "You don't think it could be anyone
from the bank?"

"Not to my knowledge, but then that's not the sort of thing you
would tell your Human Resources representative. Have *you* told
anyone at the bank about finding her body? I'm thinking about
your safety here, although I can't think of any motive from anyone
at the bank."

"No, I haven't, well, except for Kathy, the other trainer, who I'm
sure I can trust, and Gina in Mortgages, but she's gone. Can you
keep this personal and not put it in my file or tell Rick?"

Bob frowned. "Lots of people could know by now. Of course,
it didn't happen on bank property, and it had nothing to do with
bank business. There's no reason for me to mention it in your file.
I can't help thinking, though, that you've been walking around with
this for two weeks now and there's been no resolution. It must be
very stressful. As far as I know, no one's been caught, have they?"

"Right. I've been doing a little investigating on my own. I've
talked to Alicia's brother Greg, and the customer service rep she sat
next to, but I haven't learned anything of consequence. However,
I had a disturbing phone call."

"What about?"

"Detective Eastlake said I'm a suspect because my name is on
the Band of Owls membership list."

"And, of course, you're not a member, right?"

"No!"

"Then you're just a red herring for the police to follow. And perhaps they want to make you nervous too."

"Well, they've succeeded."

"I can also tell you," Bob continued, "that I know what happened with Howdy Evans the other day. Poor guy."

Emily explained to Melinda and Elvis about Howdy's mental breakdown at work.

"That's so sad," Melinda said. "Grief can affect people in funny ways."

"I have friends who work at the Rockford Center," Elvis offered. "If he winds up there, he's in good hands. They offer both inpatient and outpatient services."

"Human Resources can always work with him," Bob offered. "That's my field," he said, by way of explanation, nodding to Elvis. "What's yours?"

"I'm a writer. I do technical manuals for a variety of software companies. I get to work from home, which I love."

"Do you have a degree for that?" Bob asked.

"Yes, but it's one of those fields that changes every day. I'm constantly learning new stuff. You can't stop researching or you'll get left behind."

"I need to keep updating my computer skills, too, just for human resource management," Bob agreed.

The Belin Café was located on Workers Hill, so after lunch, they strolled down to the powder mills that were located on the banks of the Brandywine River. This was the area where the duPonts had produced gunpowder starting in 1802. It was the scene of many deaths, when a stray spark would ignite the powder and cause an explosion, killing or injuring any workers in a powder mill. In her enjoyment of the fair and the company of her friends, Emily had totally forgotten about Melinda's gift. Now, as they approached the stone buildings along the banks of the Brandywine, she remembered Melinda's vision of Corey petting the horses and probably being killed in an explosion. As they started down the path toward the river, Melinda suddenly stopped, then grabbed her stomach, leaned over a nearby bush, and was sick.

Elvis put his arms around her shoulders. "Was the pizza bad?" he asked. "Are you okay?"

"All the men. I'm seeing all the men. So many men killed and maimed. Right here. On these grounds."

Melinda sunk down on her knees and put her head in her hands. "I don't want to see them," she said. "I can't help them. There's too many of them."

"What is she talking about?" Bob asked. "I don't see any men."

"Remember I told you Melinda has a bit of ESP. She's a clairsentient, and sometimes she is seeing or sensing the spirits of the dead," Emily explained.

"That's right; you did tell me," Bob nodded his head.

Emily caught a quick look that passed between the two men, almost as if they were embarrassed that they had been caught out dating a couple of crazy old ladies. Emily didn't know how much Melinda had confided in Elvis about her second sight. Emily herself had never doubted Melinda because of the numerous past experiences where her visions had proven to be reliable, and the fact that the other ninety-nine percent of her personality was so spot-on down-to-earth.

Men, however, could be very tuned into the persona of the masculine ideal, and having a girlfriend who communed with the dead could be seen as very uncool. Would Elvis reevaluate his opinion of Melinda based on a possible negative opinion Bob had of him? Emily was worried.

"Does this happen often?" Bob asked.

"Luckily, no," Elvis said. "I call her My Lady of Second Sight. She is the most fascinating person I know. I envy her, her gift."

Emily was flooded with feelings of relief. He'd defended Melinda. She hoped Bob would be as understanding.

"Can you get her something?" Elvis said to Emily as he continued to comfort Melinda. "Maybe go back to the café and get a Coke or Sprite, something cold with some caffeine or sugar?"

"Of course."

"I'll stay here in case you need me to get more help," Bob offered. "Maybe you can explain more of this to me while we're waiting for Emily."

Emily started back up the path, passing on her right a yellow wood building that she remembered from a previous tour. It had housed the business office for the gunpowder products.

As she passed the low entrance to its first floor, a man reached out and grabbed her, pulling her inside and slamming shut the windowless door. With one arm he clamped her to his chest, and with the other covered her mouth. It was dark in the building, probably because it was not in use that day. Emily could smell rotted wood and musty clothes. She struggled to get a look at the man who held her, unable to discern much in the half-light coming in from another room. She finally guessed it was Wyatt, partially from the smell of marijuana.

"What are you up to?" he hissed in her ear, relaxing his hand enough for her mouth to form words.

"I'm just here with my friends, enjoying the fair," she said. "What are *you* doing here?"

"Oh, a little bird told me you'd be here. I want to know why you're snooping around Greg and the Owls."

Emily hesitated to answer. To tell him she was investigating Alicia's death might be the wrong thing to say.

"I found her body. I saw the tattoo. I'm just curious what happened to her."

"And what have you found out?"

"Nothing. I haven't found out anything. Do you know something?"

"Bah, you're a stupid old lady," he said and flung her away from him and further back into the darkened room. She fell and landed on her rear end. She noted gratefully that there was no crack of broken bones; fifty-something bones broke easily. That's all she needed was to be stuck in this deserted building, in the dark, with a broken hip.

"What are you going to do now?" she asked. "I can't help you."

"Stay away from Greg Kingston," he said.

"What about Rick? Is he involved?"

"That bastard can take care of himself," Wyatt growled and left, slamming the door behind him, leaving Emily alone on the floor. She gingerly got up, went to the door, and let herself out with no trouble.

There was no time to sit and ponder the meaning of Wyatt's warnings; Melinda needed something cold to drink. Emily continued her walk back up to the café for a soda, dusting the dirt from her clothes as she went, and limping just a little until she had walked off the slight injury to her posterior and her equanimity. Getting a can of Sprite, she took it down to Melinda and Elvis. They were now sitting on a low stone wall along the path through the powder yard.

Melinda took the soda gratefully and seemed to revive a bit after

just a few sips. She sat up straighter and took some deep breaths.
"Was it crowded?" Elvis asked, referring to the amount of time
it had taken Emily to return.
"I saw Wyatt," she said.
"Who's Wyatt?" Bob frowned.
"Someone connected with Alicia's murder," Emily explained.
"I'm not sure who he is or what his role is, but he keeps turning up,
like now." She went on to explain what had just happened.
"You're onto something," Melinda said. "He's scared."
"Exactly," echoed Elvis. "But you must be careful."
"Yes...please," Bob agreed.
When Melinda felt better, they returned to the fair. Emily
and Melinda each found a pair of earrings, but the guys became
increasingly bored as they wandered from one craft display to the
next. After two hours, Elvis said he needed a change of scene.
Since they were perhaps only a mile or so away from Brandywine
Creek State Park, Elvis said he was interested in seeing the spot
where Melinda and Emily had found Alicia's body. The foursome
leisurely made their way through the warm autumn sunshine back
to the RAV4. Melinda was walking confidently on her own now,
totally recovered from her earlier experience. Emily went with Bob
in his car and met Melinda and Elvis at the park.
On the grounds this sunny afternoon, there was a crowd of people,
walking dogs and playing with children. Slowly the couples made
their way up the path in the direction of the Hawk Watch, stopping at
the break in the low stone wall. In this spot, they were alone.
The sun chose that moment to slide behind a cloud, and a cool
breeze kicked up, scattering leaves into a swirl around the fallen
tree where the body had lain. The police tape and been rehung, and
the dirty yellow and black ribbon dangled from tree branches and
bushes, circling the spot where they had found Alicia's body. The
landscape had settled back into its casual unkept state of emaciated
bushes, orphaned branches, and unmowed grass. For all the happy
shouting of nearby children and calls to "Be careful" from concerned
parents, this spot seemed desolate and remote. Not a final resting
place of anyone's choosing.
"Let's sit," suggested Melinda, and they went to the stone wall
that was neatly piled up to about three feet off the ground. They
all sat down on its uneven surface. The stones were cold, but that
discomfort seemed only fitting for the tragedy that had taken place

just yards away. The air they breathed felt thick with suffering and suspicion. They each squirmed uncomfortably, thoughts of murder and motives swirling in their brains.

"I wish I could remember more about her," Bob said. "But I see hundreds of people in my office, and she never came to me with a complaint or a problem."

"I got an anonymous phone call warning me about you," Emily said, mistaking the haunting grief of the murder scene for her misgivings about Bob. She thought telling him might help clear the air. She'd enjoyed his company so far. She didn't want to keep secrets.

"What did they say?" he asked.

"Only that you weren't what you seemed."

"I don't know what they could mean by that."

"Are you married?" Melinda asked.

"No. I'm divorced. No children."

"Are *you* a member of the Band of Owls?" Emily asked.

"No, I'm not a member."

"I've read about them," Elvis said. "They're supposed to be a secret organization, very antitechnology, or anti-industry. Maybe both. I'm not sure."

"Perhaps you're investigating me," Emily said, not to be distracted by Elvis.

"No, I'm not," Bob replied. "It would be unethical for me to be here with you today if I were. A part of me is offended that you would question me, but I understand that if you've been threatened, then you need to be careful. I can look out for you."

"I don't want anyone looking out for me," Emily replied, trying not to sound haughty. "I can usually take care of myself."

"I admire that. I take back my offer," he said and grinned. There was nothing to be gained by taking offense.

"No hard feelings?" he added

"No." Emily smiled at him. The awkward moment passed. Her gloom lifted. She didn't know why, but she wanted to trust him. The past few hours had been stressful with Melinda being sick, Wyatt's attack, and her suspicions. She didn't have Melinda's second sight, but she thought Bob's answers had been honest. She felt herself relax.

"Heh, what shall we do for dinner?" Melinda interrupted. "I'm hungry again."

"There's the Pit. What do you say?" Elvis offered.

"'The Pit,'" Melinda echoed. "Do I want to eat somewhere called 'The Pit'?"

"It's perfect for a day when you're dressed in jeans and sneakers," Emily explained. "They're famous for their burgers and fries, but more importantly, they make milkshakes with real milk. You'll love it. What do you say, Bob?"

"One of my favorites."

En masse they got up from the stone wall and headed back down the hill toward the parking lot.

At the Charcoal Pit, they squeezed into a booth and fidgeted with the jukebox selections, most from the sixties. Back in the day, this had been *the* hangout after high school dances. Emily had rarely dated in the crowd that hung out there, but she and her girlfriends had occasionally come to share one of the enormous Pit sundaes, which were named after the local high school football teams. Emily's favorite had been the Sallies, named after the local boy's high school, Salesianum, the school her occasional dates attended. The sundae had four scoops of vanilla and chocolate ice cream, butterscotch topping, marshmallow cream, whipped cream, and a cherry. It took four girls to eat one—four girls who had thrown their diets to the wind for the evening, perhaps because one was suffering from a broken heart while the others ate in sympathy.

This day, the foursome ordered burgers and fries. The guys opted for shakes: chocolate for Bob and vanilla for Elvis, and Melinda and Emily ordered Diet Cokes. Waiting for their order, Emily reminisced, "Boy does this place bring back memories. I haven't been here in at least ten, maybe twenty years. It hasn't changed one bit."

Suddenly the jukebox kicked on and the Beatles were singing, "Try and see it my way…" Emily was plunged into memories of an old boyfriend she'd let slip away. She hadn't "seen it his way" and gone on to marry someone else who'd later broken her heart.

"Would you want to go back and relive that carefree time?" Bob asked, in all innocence.

"Carefree?" Melinda choked on her first sip of Coke. "Not my adolescence. I was six feet tall when I was fourteen. My life was hell. How 'bout you, Em."

"I was pretty but dumb as a brick. I made a million wrong choices. I would *not* want to go back to that."

"I was fat," Elvis offered, and they all laughed in astonishment as he was trim and athletic now.

"Looks like we're all just as happy to be who we are," Bob observed. "I guess it makes up for the lines and the wrinkles."

Emily felt a sudden chill as she thought of Alicia who would never know the joys of old age.

CHAPTER TWENTY-SEVEN
THERE HAVE BEEN BETTER DAYS

Emily spent Monday morning working on a new training manual. She didn't see Rick in his office, Kathy had a training class, and the floor in general seemed to be enjoying a lull of order and quiet. Emily found it restful.

At lunchtime, she called Bob's office to see if he was free but was told he was out for the day. Funny, she thought, he hadn't mentioned anything about being gone for an entire day.

She decided to grab a sandwich in the cafeteria and was dismayed to find no one she knew to share her lunch with, so she sat at a small table near the window and did a crossword puzzle while she ate chicken salad on rye and drank a small bottle of cranberry juice.

She glanced outside at the trees, which were now dropping their leaves and looking as desolate as she felt. She thought of Alicia and her young life so violently taken from her against her will and thought that she herself should feel grateful to be alive, but it was a hollow feeling without friends or coworkers to share that life with this chilly autumn afternoon. She thought of Howdy suffering through his grief at the Rockford Center and Greg preparing to be homeless at the end of the month. Now feeling completely depressed, she gathered up her lunch garbage and deposited it in the trash.

After taking the elevator back to the tenth floor, she stopped in to the lady's room. While sitting on the john and contemplating the cheapness of the toilet paper that the bank provided, she heard two women enter who immediately began talking about Kathy's training class.

"Thank god we have her and not that other nitwit who hasn't a clue what this job is about," tittered one woman over the sounds of running faucets and paper towels being pulled.

Emily froze. Were they talking about her?

"At least Kathy has done this job before. I can't stand a trainer who doesn't know what it's like to talk to these people on the phone. Why did they hire her?"

They *were* talking about her. Emily didn't move as she listened to them finish their washing up.

"Emily came from the bank we bought in New Hampshire where they didn't have corporate clients."

She heard the door open.

"Well, I wish they'd send her back there. She's useless here."

The door closed with a swish, and the two women were gone. Emily put her face in her hands. Was the entire department laughing at her? Had this gotten back to Rick? And worse yet, had it gotten back to Bob in Human Resources? How could it not?

She pulled herself together, washed her hands, and left the bathroom. Returning to her desk, she signed back in to her computer and stared at her email without reading any of it. She felt like such a fool. It had been a mistake to come back here to Wilmington. Her old friends didn't have time for her. She was a failure at her job. She'd gotten herself engaged to a man she didn't love. Worst of all, she had no other place else to live. Could life get any worse?

Well, she would have to show them that she could learn. She pulled up the training manual she was working on and decided she needed to have someone with experience review what she'd done so far. She printed out a copy and wrote a note to Kathy: "Could you please review this for accuracy? I know you're busy with a class now, so take your time and make all the notes you want. I realize I've never done this job myself, so I want to be sure I've got the material correct."

She left the document on Kathy's desk, feeling marginally better since she had at least taken a positive step in correcting her deficiency. She decided to spend the rest of the afternoon answering email.

At five o'clock she shut down her computer and headed out of the office. She was still feeling a bit down, so she stopped at Boscov's on the way home and did a little shopping. A new purse and pair of soft leather gloves later, she was feeling a bit perkier as she pulled into the driveway of Desmond's home. She let herself in the door, hoping to be greeted by the aroma of dinner on the stove.

"Where the hell have you been?" Desmond growled, a glass of

brown liquid in one hand and a large cooking fork in the other. His face was red with anger. His dark eyes hard as stone.

"I stopped to do some shopping." Emily held up her bag.

Whoosh! The fork flew in front of her face and hooked on the bag handle, flinging the bag across the room.

"You knew I'd have dinner waiting."

"No, I didn't. Sometimes we don't eat until six-thirty or seven." She was frightened now. She took a step backward toward the door she'd just entered.

"You know how important having dinner on time is to me," he growled again. The growl was scarier than if he'd raised his voice. It was feral, like a cornered animal.

"Honestly, I never noticed. We seem to have dinner at different times on different days," Emily said, half hating herself for being conciliatory, but Desmond was obviously drunk and irrational.

"No, we don't!" Now he did raise his voice, and with it, he raised the fork again. His face had gone beyond red to purple, his eyes bulged. Emily was sure he was going to hit her if he didn't have a stroke first. One thing she knew for sure, she was not staying around to see which it was. Without a word, she turned and ran out the door. Shaking so hard she could hardly hold on to the keys still in her hands, she managed to unlock the car door and get in, slam it shut, and lock the doors. She looked up. She didn't see Desmond but decided not to wait around to see if he would follow her. She started the car and backed out of the driveway, then sped up the street, looking into the rearview mirror once or twice to make sure he hadn't decided to follow her.

She was shaking and distracted, hardly able to focus on the road, as she drove into Wilmington to the DoubleTree Hotel where Melinda had stayed when she visited. She kept seeing Desmond's angry face and the fork raised as if to strike her. He'd never behaved like this before. Perhaps he'd had a bad day at work too and started drinking earlier than usual.

She drove down the ramp into the parking garage of the hotel, found an empty space, parked, and locked her car. The dimly lit garage was a bit confusing in her troubled state, but she finally found the elevators and ascended to the lobby.

She was still trembling when she approached the desk clerk and asked for a room. The desk clerk showed no reaction to a single woman with no luggage taking a room for the night, not even when

Emily asked for a toothbrush, which the desk clerk provided for free. Next, Emily went up to her room, sat on the bed, and took a series of deep breaths. What had just happened? Desmond had threatened her, and she'd had to leave. Never, ever, had she imagined herself on the receiving end of domestic violence. Yet here she was, alone in a hotel room, having fled from an abusive boyfriend. She was proud of herself, though. Without thinking she'd taken herself out of danger. She hadn't tried to reason with him or defend herself. She'd merely left, and that had been the right thing to do. She hugged herself, rubbing her hands up and down both arms as if trying to warm them. Slowly, with continued deep breaths, the shaking lessened.

As she felt herself calming down, she found the narrow binder with a list of the hotel's amenities, picked up the phone, and ordered a cheese and crackers plate along with a carafe of white wine. Then she found Elvis's home phone number—the home where Melinda was now staying, maybe indefinitely—and called.

When Elvis answered he seemed happy to hear Emily and asked how she was.

"I've been better," she sighed. "Can I speak to Melinda?"

She told her the whole story, from her lonely lunch to the women in the ladies' room to Desmond's threatening behavior.

"How are you coping? Have you been crying?"

"I don't feel anything right now. I feel numb."

"You're in shock. It won't last."

"I can't believe what a fool I've been," Emily said. "It will be hard enough to go back to work. I can't go back to Desmond's."

"Of course, you can't. You can come and stay here with Elvis and me. Just let me clear it with him. Hold on."

"Wait, wait, wait!"

"What?"

"Tell him only until I find an apartment."

"I'll tell him, but I'd love to have you here always."

"Thank you, but Elvis might feel differently."

In a minute Melinda was back on the phone. "He would be thrilled to have two lovely ladies share his humble abode and can't wait for his ex to hear about it. Do you want to come over tonight?"

"No, I need some alone time tonight. I've already booked this room and ordered wine and cheese, so I'll be fine, but thank you so much. And tell Elvis how much I appreciate it. I'll start looking for a place this weekend. I should have gotten my own place right from the beginning."

"You ran into an old love and were happy for the friendship and the company. I would have done the same thing. Don't beat yourself up over living with Des."

"I like to think of myself as being strong and independent, but in the long run, I never am, am I?"

"Of course, you are. Lots of women would have stuck it out with him because they were afraid of going out on their own. You didn't think twice. You hotfooted it out of there before he could hurt you. I think you are smart and brave."

"I love you, Melinda. You always make me feel better."

"That's my job."

"I'll call you tomorrow."

"And you move in tomorrow night."

"I will."

Emily hung up the phone and waited to cry. She was surprised that tears didn't come. Instead, she felt nothing. She sat quietly and searched within herself for feelings. She was aware that she should be devastated, and angry, and maybe even a bit apprehensive about the future. What she felt was not any of that. She felt like she inhabited a void, an empty space. She felt like an astronaut who had stepped outside of her spaceship and was floating in the vastness of space. There was no earth beneath her feet and nothing to ground her. She was tethered to existence by only a thin cord that stretched to a spaceship, and that spaceship was her world, from which it would take only the slightest tug to disconnect, and then off she would go, spinning into the emptiness of the cosmos forever.

Sitting on the hotel bed alone, she felt the coldness and isolation of space. It wasn't someplace she wanted to be. She heard a voice in her head saying, "Don't make such a fuss. Just shake it off and get on with it."

Her thoughts were interrupted by a knock at the hotel room door. Jolted out of her reverie, she answered it and saw the bellhop with her food. She gave him a five-dollar tip and sat down again on the bed, forgetting her previous feelings of detachment. She was hungry now. She turned on the news and contemplated the practicalities of her situation. She would have to go to work tomorrow in the same clothes she had on today, but she doubted anyone would notice. She hadn't even spoken to anyone in her department that day.

At lunchtime, when Desmond would be at work, she would let herself into his house and quickly gather up all her clothes and toiletries and pile them in her car. She'd leave him a note of explanation. After work, she would drive out to Elvis's home.

Thank goodness for the balm of Bacchus. Emily was asleep by ten, tired enough to ignore a small nagging voice suggesting that she was planning to live with yet another unknown man.

Less than a mile away, two men relaxed on worn leather Barcaloungers enjoying glasses of Johnnie Walker Red. They were silent for a moment, savoring their drinks, listening to the clink of ice cubes as they meditated on what they were planning.

The room was paneled in a buttery walnut. The track lighting dimmed to cast only meager beams on a scattering of Wyeth prints. The dark drapes were pulled back to show off the built-in brick barbeque on the outdoor patio surrounded by carefully landscaped shrubs and lit with solar spotlights.

The neat brick home sat midway up Bancroft Parkway, a wide boulevard on the southwest side of Wilmington. At the northern end of the Parkway were two-story row homes split into upper and lower apartments known as "the flats." Bancroft Parkway was named for William Bancroft who established The Woodlawn Company in 1901, later known as Woodlawn Trustees. The residences were built to provide housing for working-class people of modest means. In 2000, they were still popular rental units for young families and provided attractive, low-cost housing on the edge of the city within walking distance of restaurants, shops, and bus stops.

Driving south along the boulevard the homes morphed into several blocks of middle-class Georgian brick domiciles, and at the far southern end into impressive stone minimansions with half-acre plots. Bancroft Parkway was a desirable address for those of all income levels.

In between the north and south-flowing traffic lanes was a twenty-yard expanse of shaded green parkland meticulously groomed every spring but run to dust at summer's end by the horde of jittery kids from the flats.

"Let's review," Rick said, putting down his glass. "You've put it out that the computer virus attack will be in December, but it's actually scheduled for later this month."

"Correct," Wyatt replied, taking another sip of his scotch. "And I'm not telling you when, so you can't be compromised. The bank's not sending you out of town any time soon?"

"No, no. I'll be here. I wouldn't mind being prepared."

"You'll know the moment you arrive at work. All the computers will be down, and I imagine your staff will be running around like chickens with their heads cut off. We'll need most of the day for our bugs to do their work. Then you can step in at the end of the day and play the savior to get the system back online, but the data will be gone."

"Sweet. I've got two mortgages and twenty thou in credit card debt myself. Not to mention a car loan."

"I'm worried about someone spilling the beans. What do you think about Howdy?"

"Not a problem. He's at Rockford Center now, and when he gets out, I've got him in such a sexual tizzy he doesn't know if he's gay or bi or something else entirely. He's not even thinking about this hack job."

"What about that woman who keeps sticking her nose in everyone's business?"

"Emily? My trainer?"

"Yeah. I've been keeping tabs on her. She's been talking to Greg and Howdy, and I'm worried Greg may have let on what we're planning."

"Don't worry about her. I've given her a huge assignment and hinted her job depends on it. She's also cozying up to a guy in Human Resources, but I don't think he's a problem. I've got a little reverse psychology going on there, so what with her training project and her Romeo and Juliet fantasies, I don't think she'll have any time to do any more research on the Owls."

Wyatt rose to leave. "Thanks for the drinks, bro."

"Anytime. You just do your job. I'll do mine. Next time I see you, we'll be laughing our asses off."

CHAPTER TWENTY-EIGHT
A Better Day

When Emily awoke Tuesday morning, she used the ironing board she found in the hotel room closet to carefully iron her clothes, hoping to make them look as fresh as possible. After her shower, she dressed and checked out of her room, arriving at work at seven-thirty. No one had arrived, so she went down to the cafeteria for a leisurely breakfast. She chose her usual cranberry and orange muffin and a cup of hot coffee. Sitting alone at a small table near the window, she sipped her coffee and watched the trees dropping their leaves onto the gray cement patio outside. Inside, she was still numb to the happenings of the last evening. She was operating on autopilot.

"You're here early," Bob greeted her, balancing a muffin and coffee of his own. "Mind if I join you?"

"Please do," Emily smiled, pleased to start her day with at least one friendly face at the bank.

"This is my normal morning routine," he continued. "I've never seen you down here this early. Trouble sleeping?"

"I had a disagreement with my roommate and spent last night at the DoubleTree Hotel. I don't think I'll be going back there except to pick up my clothes. I need to look for my own place. In the meantime, I'll move in with Elvis and Melinda."

"Some disagreement. Were you physically hurt in any way?"

"No. You might as well know. He was an old boyfriend from high school that I reconnected with when the bank offered me the job here in Wilmington. It was a wrong decision. He's developed a drinking problem and last night he lost his temper. He never actually touched me, but the threat was there. I'm not stupid enough to think it'll never happen again. I walked out, and thankfully, he didn't try to follow me."

"I'm sorry. You told me you were divorced and that you recently broke up with a man in New Hampshire. You seem to be going through a bad patch. Do these experiences make you less willing to trust men in general?"

"I'm afraid I'm hopelessly optimistic." Emily smiled, thinking you could also interpret that as "I'm not too bright"—which Bob might have been doing.

"I like optimistic people," he replied. They ate and drank coffee in comfortable silence for a few moments until Bob spoke.

"I have a realtor friend, Lou Champion, who knows every apartment, condo, and home on the market in New Castle County. Would you like his phone number? He's one of the few realtors I'd trust with family."

"As I don't know anyone, I'd love his number. Send me an email when you get back to your desk."

"I'll call him to let him know you're a friend. Why don't we have lunch and you can tell me how your call to him went?"

"I can't do that. I've got to get my clothes from my friend's house. He'll be at work then. I don't want to go after work and risk a confrontation."

"Would you like me to go with you?"

"No, I'll be fine."

"What if you see his car in the driveway?"

"I won't go in. I'll go shopping and get a new outfit instead. No hardship there."

Breakfasts finished, they pushed back their chairs to go.

"A drink after work, then?" Bob asked.

"Okay. O'Friel's?"

"It's a date."

They walked in companionable silence to the elevators.

Around eleven, Emily called the number for the realtor and was pleasantly surprised to hear him answer the phone himself, rather than a secretary or voicemail. She introduced herself as Bob's friend, Emily.

"Bob said you were looking for an apartment, are you sure I couldn't interest you in a condo or a town house? The market's good."

"I'd love to buy—maybe a condo. But I'm not sure I can afford it." Thinking of Paradise Found, she added, "The last thing I want is to lose my home to foreclosure."

Lou asked her about her salary and savings and said he was confident they could find something that wouldn't deplete her savings or overstretch her paycheck. This was cheering news to Emily.

"I think you could afford something between sixty and seventy-five thousand dollars," he said.

"Are there any condos in that price range?" she asked. Suddenly Emily felt that she wanted to put down roots. She didn't want to rent. She wanted to own. She didn't want to ever be in a position of being forced out of her home again.

"What area?" Lou asked. "There are some nice homes in the Newark area, off Route 896. Are you sure you don't want a house?"

"Well, I want to be sure I don't buy more than I can afford. Let's stick to condos."

The community he had in mind was inexpensive but in a quiet family neighborhood. They made an appointment for 10 a.m. on Saturday morning. When Emily put down the receiver, she was feeling better than she had in days. Tuesday was certainly a better day than Monday had been.

At twelve, she went to her car and headed to Desmond's home. It was going to take more than her hour lunch to get there, pack her clothes, and return to work, but she'd been in early, so the time should even itself out. Nonetheless, she was worried as she drove her car into Desmond's development.

His car was not in sight. She backed her car up the driveway and stopped as she thought about how to hide her activities from the neighbors. She glanced in the windows of the garage and was relieved to find one side empty. Desmond's Miata was gone, although the truck was still there. She let herself in, then went into the garage and raised the door. Then she backed her car in and lowered the doors. With her car hidden in the garage, she could pack it up without anyone seeing her. Desmond had lived in this development for over twenty years. Who knew which stay-at-home mom might be looking out her window, think that someone was stealing, and call Desmond at work. The last thing Emily wanted was another scene.

She opened the passenger doors of her car and then went upstairs to the closet where she gathered armfuls of clothes and brought them down to the car. After several trips, she found her luggage and filled the suitcases with the clothes in the dresser drawers and with toiletries from the bathroom. With each trip down the stairs, she had glanced anxiously out the house windows for a car coming down the street. If Desmond arrived and pulled in the driveway, she'd be trapped.

As the hour went by, her nerves became more jangled, and she was visibly trembling with fright that Desmond would arrive and…do what? Her mind pictured various reactions as she lugged armfuls of clothing to the car. Ask her to stay? Probably not. Berate her for leaving? More likely. Call her names? Possibly. Make her feel stupid for having trusted him? For sure.

By her final trip, she was sweating furiously both from exertion and anxiety.

After packing the car, she thought about the few kitchen utensils, and pots and pans, that she'd brought with her from New Hampshire. Most had been remnants from her ten-year marriage. He could have them, she decided. She could replace them all at the Goodwill store.

In a corner of the kitchen, she found her Boscov's bag from the night before, lying where Desmond had flung it with his fork. She retrieved it and bid a silent farewell to the kitchen in which she and Desmond had shared so many happy meals. Her last gesture was to leave a carefully prepared note on the table:

Dear Des,

Your angry outburst frightened me last night, and I've decided that I can't live here any longer. In the past few days we have grown distant and I've noticed that you spend every evening in your den drinking. I think I was unwise to accept your offer of marriage, and have decided that we should not marry, and that I would prefer not to see you again. I've taken all my clothes and will not be back. You are welcome to any kitchen items I've left behind. Please do not call me or try to contact me. I wish you happiness in the future. I just don't think I can share that future with you.

Emily

With some relief, she realized she had never given him Melinda's phone number and had never mentioned where Elvis lived. She should be safe from retaliation, if indeed he was that sort of person. It was a measure of how little she knew him that she couldn't answer that question for herself.

She moved the car out of the garage and went back inside to put down the garage door. As she went through the screened-in porch where she had enjoyed sitting so much, she stole a last glimpse at the golden glow of the colors of the backyard trees.

"I'll miss you," she whispered to the house. "But someday I'll have a place of my own."

When she got back to work, all was quiet. Emily found the training packet she'd left on Kathy's desk the day before now sitting on her own desk with a note, "Looks good. Just a few updates I'll speak to you about later. Kath."

Feeling better than she had for the past twenty-four hours, Emily went down to the cafeteria and picked up a roast beef sandwich to go and the usual bottle of cranberry juice. As she was heading for the exit, she saw Bob, seated alone at a table.

"Hi," she said and stopped at his seat, noticing a half-eaten salad and large slice of apple pie. "Interesting lunch combo."

"Hi! Have a seat. Did you get your errand done?"

She sat down and sighed. "Yes, and thank goodness no one saw me."

"Stay and keep me company."

"Can't. It's two o'clock already. But I'll see you at five, right?"

"Yes, and oh, I wanted you to know that there's an opening for a loan administrator in Global Loans. Almost no telephone work. Just receiving faxes and email requests for money and then sending that money out on the computer. Interested? It's eight thirty to five, Monday to Friday. They're a nice group to work with."

"I haven't been in my present position long enough to apply for something else."

"I might be able to help with that. Shall I see if I can get you an interview?"

"I'd love it. Gotta go." Emily got up from her seat and headed toward the exit. Fifty-something banking women should not be seen skipping across the cafeteria floor, but Emily could have done it anyway.

When she returned to her desk, she decided that it had been a good enough day that she could risk some bad news. She called Detective Eastlake for an update on the investigation into Alicia's murder. The detective picked up on the first ring.

"We've had quite a few people in for questioning," she reported. "I'm not at liberty to give you their names. The person who told us that you were a member of the Owls has rescinded that information, so we're no longer looking at you as a possible suspect." *More good news,* thought Emily, although she had never been able to take the allegation seriously.

"No arrests?" Emily asked.

"No arrests," Eastlake confirmed. "I'll let you know when there is."

"Thank you."

Emily's next call was to Melinda. "I successfully retrieved my clothes from Desmond's," she reported.

"Wonderful. Will you come here straight after work?"

"I'm meeting Bob for a drink. Don't include me in your dinner plans. I'll stop at the Acme for some cereal and crackers and stuff. I'm a big believer in cereal for dinner."

"We'll have some leftovers for you. How are you feeling?"

"Unsettled. But I supposed that feeling's going to last until I have my own place."

"Try not to worry about it. Everything will work out. You made the right decision." The everyday assurances were nonetheless comforting.

"Thank you. See you later."

Detective Eastlake was ready to leave for the day when one of the desk sergeants knocked on her door.

"Someone left an envelope for you," the sergeant said. "We checked it out. It's a cassette tape. No name anywhere. Just the instructions to give it to you."

"Leave it on the desk," Eastlake said and put down her purse. Looked like she wasn't leaving just yet.

CHAPTER TWENTY-NINE

New Beginnings

When Emily entered O'Friel's that evening, there was no ghostly presence at the door or scent of freshly shampooed hair. There was, instead, the odor of stale cigarettes and spilled beer. Emily was just a tad disappointed. She found Bob already ensconced in a tall booth with a mug of his favorite. He raised his hand to her.

"Good news," he said as she settled in across from him "You have an interview with John Joseph next Tuesday at four in the afternoon for the Loan Administrator position, unless that time is inconvenient." He handed her one of his business cards with John's name and telephone number printed on the plain side. "Just call him and reschedule if you need to."

"How did you pull this off?"

"I told them your skills were uniquely suited for the job and that I hadn't found any other candidates more qualified."

"Do you know what my skills are?"

"I'm in Human Resources, remember?"

"No offense, Bob, but it worries me just a little to have you pull strings for me when we don't even know each other that well."

"Believe me, Emily, I've got the bank's interests in mind. You are the best candidate. You just don't know it."

"Are you sure?"

The waiter arrived, and their conversation paused long enough for Emily to order a glass of wine.

"An order of mozzarella sticks too," Bob added. With a nod, the waiter departed.

"Emily, let's review your employment assets. You always arrive to work on time and stay at least until quitting time. You rarely call in sick or ask for last-minute time off. How much time do you spend standing in the aisles talking to coworkers?"

"Not much. A few minutes a day."

"How much time do you spend on the telephone each day talking to friends and family?"

"Almost none."

"Listen, we have employees who are absent at least once a week for a different reason each time. We have employees who spend forty-five minutes at a time hanging out in someone else's cubicle just to gossip. We have employees who make two hours' worth of personal phone calls every day. You are a gold star employee compared to them."

"I'm sure you must have other gold star employees. Doesn't Mirety always hire the best and the brightest?"

"I'll tell you a secret, but don't spread it around. We aren't trying to be the best. We're perfectly content with second or third place. We don't want to pay our employees enough to be the best."

"Wow, that's a morale builder. Now I know why I'm still here," she laughed. "But there's also skill matching."

Her wine arrived, and she took a grateful sip. With one taste, her body seemed to go limp all over. What a stressful two days it had been. Hopefully, there would be no more challenges, other than her job interview next week.

"Yes, skill matching." Bob took a sip of his beer and accepted a plate of mozzarella sticks from the waiter. He offered them to Emily who helped herself to one. After taking one himself, he continued, "Your file states that you've passed two bank-sponsored courses in accounting. Remember them?"

"Oh, yes! That was two years ago. I can't do geometry, but I'm good at accounting."

"There you go. Your accounting skills, along with everything else I've mentioned, are what make you perfect for the Loan Administrator job. The only bad news is that it's a lateral move and you won't be getting a raise."

"I can live with that. Thank you."

"Just doin' my job, ma'am," he mugged and doffed an imaginary cowboy hat.

When Emily arrived at Elvis's home around seven thirty, she gratefully accepted his and Melinda's help unloading her car and carrying her stuff upstairs to a guest bedroom. It took only a few trips with all their help. When she had unpacked a few things and put her toiletries in the hall bath, she joined them downstairs to watch TV.

"I feel so strange," she said. "Out of place and out of time. At my age, I should be a doddering old lady baking cookies for the grandbabies. Here I am, however, no grandpa on the horizon and traipsing around between other people's homes like a gypsy with no roots."

"We're your family now," Melinda said, leaving Elvis to come over to where Emily was sitting. She leaned over her chair and gave her a hug. "I'm too old to provide substitute grandbabies, but maybe there'll be grandpuppies or kittens. What do you say, Elvis?"

"Maybe both."

"What do you both think of Bob?" Emily asked. "I don't know that I'm in a hurry to pursue another relationship, but maybe he'll be content to just date with no, uh, benefits, for a few months." She grinned at her use of the euphemism for sex.

"He seems like a straight-up good guy," Elvis offered.

"What about his aura, Mel? What did you see?"

"His was blue, like yours is sometimes. Blue means calm, caring, and intuitive. I think you're perfect for each other."

"What a relief!" Emily hugged Melinda, then added, "Well, I'm tired." She spent just a few more minutes with the couple to be polite, then excused herself and went to bed. The wine and cheese sticks had been enough dinner in her agitated emotional state. Now exhaustion was taking over, and she just wanted to sleep. She fell gratefully into the soft double bed with plaid flannel sheets. As she lay there, she started to say a prayer of thanks to whatever gods had put Bob in her path, and then admonished herself. *Silly woman, you don't need a man to rescue you. You're going to rescue yourself.* Then she fell quickly to sleep.

CHAPTER THIRTY

HOME

On Saturday, Emily met Lou Champion, the realtor, in the parking lot outside of the 9900 building of Stones Throw in Newark, Delaware. These were one and two-bedroom condos for sale costing from thirty-five to sixty-five thousand dollars. With a few thousand left over from her relocation package, she thought she could afford a down payment on one of these apartment-style units. On the outside, they were a dull-brown brick with mustard trim, not her idea of attractive, but the neighborhood appeared cared for and safe.

Promptly at ten, a black Lincoln Town Car cruised into the parking lot, and a gray-haired gentleman with wire-rimmed glasses climbed out. He appeared to be in his late forties or early fifties and was dressed in a dark suit and blue tie.

Emily hopped out of her car and walked toward him with her hand outstretched. "Hi, you're Lou? I'm Emily."

Lou had a warm smile. "Glad to meet you. Did you bring your checkbook?"

"Do you think we'll find a place today?"

"I'm sure of it. Let's take a look at 9904."

They walked up the cement path together. Emily waited while Lou worked the lockbox code to retrieve the key. Extracting the key, he opened the door and then stepped back to let her enter first.

What Emily noticed first was how dark it was. Heavy mocha drapes blocked the outside light at the living room window. The furniture was large and covered with matted gold blankets. *Yuck,* she thought.

Lou could see the distaste on her face.

"Let's check out the kitchen and dining area," he said, "they're only a few steps away."

There were no windows, only a galley sort of kitchen and a small Formica table with metal chairs. The appliances looked about fifteen years old, and the linoleum was stained. Emily didn't say anything; she didn't have to.

"Let's look at the bedroom," Lou said. "This is a one-bedroom unit on the market for $36,500."

Emily had to admit the price was right.

They returned to the hall that extended from the front door to the back of the unit. Lou turned on the ceiling light. Another dingy room appeared with more brown drapes and dark carpet.

"This is just too small and ugly," Emily said.

"A little white paint and tan carpeting would make a world of difference," Lou offered.

"Not enough, I'm afraid," Emily replied.

"Let's look at a two bedroom," he suggested.

They walked outside, and Emily waited while Lou locked up the condo. They went down the block a little further to a similar building whose units appeared to have more windows than the one they'd just been in.

"This is a two-bedroom listed for $55,000," Lou told her as he obtained the key from the lockbox and opened the door. Emily walked into a purple living room with blue shag carpet. There was no furniture, which was a help, and light tan curtains, but the living room was as small as the one-bedroom they had just visited. The kitchen had slightly newer appliances, but they were olive green. Lou could see he wasn't making any headway.

"Let's check out the bedrooms," he said and led her to two tiny rooms—one painted a Day-Glo pink and the other, teal. Emily guessed the windows to be facing north, which meant they received little light. She couldn't imagine herself living here.

"Sorry, Lou, even with new paint and carpet these condos are too small. I guess I'll have to look somewhere else or resign myself to an apartment. It's just that I wanted something of my own. Something no one could take away from me. A place to plant flowers and put down roots."

"I've got two more to show you that are town houses, so they have more room, but they're still condos meaning you own the interior and the association takes care of the exterior. They're just two blocks over. Let's walk and look at the neighborhood."

As they walked, Emily explained, "I don't think I can afford the town houses. They're much more expensive, aren't they?"

"Not this first one," he replied.

They arrived at a row of trim, two-story townhomes with postage stamp front yards and assigned parking spots in front of each one. They had white siding, with every other house having blue trim, and the in-between ones, red trim. They were certainly less depressing looking from the outside.

"These are two bedrooms, one and a half baths," Lou said cheerfully. Emily felt a little more hopeful.

Lou opened the door to a blue-trimmed townhome, and the odor of cat urine immediately repelled Emily. *No way,* she thought to herself, but she stepped inside anyway.

"This one is priced at $65,000," Lou offered. Holding her nose, Emily entered and followed the hallway with an eat-in kitchen on the right and large windows opening onto the parking lot. The kitchen was cheerful with white appliances and checkered linoleum. She followed Lou down the hallway to a dining room, and then down a step to a living room with patio doors that accessed a deck.

"I like the layout," she said, "but I've heard that the smell of cat urine is almost impossible to get rid of. You have to basically tear up the floor and replace it with new."

"That's why it's priced so low," Lou said. "Most of these townhomes go for more. Let's just take a quick look upstairs."

They returned to the hall, and Lou pointed out the powder room and closet next to the steps. More features Emily liked.

Upstairs were two bedrooms, one in the front of the house and one in the back. They shared a large bath.

"I like the house," Emily said. "But I'm still worried about that smell."

"One more on my list," Lou said. "Stick with me."

Emily waited while Lou locked up the house, and then they crossed the street to another row of homes and headed for the end unit.

"I think you'll like this one," Lou smiled.

When they walked in, Emily's spirits lifted. The carpeting was barely worn and a discreet tan color. The kitchen had white cabinets and new appliances. The front window, which framed a breakfast nook, was wide and covered with lace curtains. There were no disturbing odors.

When she walked back to the dining and living areas, she noticed first a small corner fireplace, then sliders to a large deck, and finally a deep bay window that bathed the room with light even on this particularly cloudy day.

"This is perfect," she said, doing a small twirl in the living room, already picturing where she'd place her furniture and photographs.

In the kitchen were printed brochures with room descriptions, measurements, and tax information. Emily picked one up and felt her heart plummet. The price listed was $84,900.

"I can't afford this," she said.

"What's your top number?" Lou asked.

"Well, if I really stretched it, I could probably go $75,000."

"This house has been on the market for four or five months. Why don't we just offer them seventy-five, tell them that's your highest and best, and see what they say?"

Her offer was more than ten percent less than they were asking. Emily feared that the sellers might be insulted. But what did she have to lose?

"Okay," she said. "But I won't get my hopes up. I'm not even positive I'll be approved for that much."

"Leave it to me," Lou said.

Later that afternoon back at Elvis's place, as Emily sat at his desk going over her bills and mourning what had happened to her dreams of a life with Desmond, the phone rang. It was Lou.

"They accepted your offer," he said. "Congratulations! I'll fax the sales contract to you this afternoon, and you can fax it back to me once you've signed. Where would you like me to send it?"

"The friend I'm staying with works from home and uses this number for calls and for faxes, so use the number you just called."

"Great! Now, where were you going to apply for a mortgage?" Lou asked.

"Probably at Mirety Bank."

"Will you do me a favor and speak to my girl first? My real estate firm also has a mortgage company. Stop in Monday evening after work. We're located at 9899 Old Capitol Trail. She's there until seven. Her name is Cynthia."

Emily was in Cynthia's office by five thirty Monday afternoon. Cynthia was thin and dark, with a charming smile and reassuring manner. When the paperwork was all done, Emily was putting down $1500, taking out a mortgage for $60,000, and a home equity loan for $13,500.

Though concerned that she was allowed to borrow such a large part of the cost, Emily trusted Cynthia that it was all legal. These were crazy times in the real estate business as she had witnessed in the Mirety Mortgages department.

CHAPTER THIRTY-ONE
Everything Goes Wrong, Again

On Tuesday morning, Emily's mood changed. When she woke up, a glance out the window revealed dark clouds flirting with the edge of the sky. The air was cold. She felt too exhausted to go to work, but there was no choice. She heaved herself out of bed and willed herself into the shower, dried herself listlessly, and bemoaned how tired her arms were as she blow-dried her hair. She understood that the recent upheaval in her living arrangement and split with Desmond was the cause of her inertia, but the knowledge alone had no restorative power. She didn't hear or see Melinda or Elvis as she crept downstairs. Not wanting to wake them, she decided to leave and grab breakfast at the bank.

When she pulled up to the bank building that morning, she knew immediately that something was wrong. She thought to herself that she'd better lose the fog in her brain and pay attention. There were security guards at the entrance to the parking garage who stopped her car before she could enter. The gate was raised, but she needed to show her employee badge to the guard. He sported a black leather holster for his exposed gun and held a walkie-talkie in his hand.

"Who's your boss?" he asked.

"Rick Wiseburg," she replied.

"Stay clear of him if you can," the guard replied, and then stood back to let her pass.

Stay clear of him? What did that mean? He was her boss. If he wanted to speak to her, he would come to her desk. Feeling a bit nauseous with the uncertainty of the guard's implication, Emily drove up to her assigned level, parked her car, entered the building, and took the elevator to her floor. She appeared to be the first to arrive on her floor. She sat at her desk and tried to power up her computer, but she couldn't. It didn't have any juice. She checked that it was plugged in and all the appropriate wires were connected. No one else had arrived yet, so she couldn't check to see if others were having the same problem. She noticed that the ceiling lights were working, and the air conditioning was humming. She figured the computers must be down for some reason. With nothing else to do, she decided to go to the cafeteria for coffee.

No one was in the hallways, and she rode down to the basement alone. As the elevator doors opened, she heard the usual hustle and bustle of trays banging and coworkers chatting coming from the cafeteria. She grabbed an orange-cranberry muffin and a black coffee.

At the checkout, the woman cashier smiled and said, "Everything okay on your floor, dear?"

"Seems to be, except the systems are down."

"All over the building, honey. Luckily, I got an old-fashioned adding machine here. But you take care. Something's not right. I feel it."

"Thank you. You take care too."

Back at her desk, Emily noticed that Rick was still not in his office. She checked her PC again, but still no power. She spread out a napkin, took a bite of muffin, and then a sip of coffee. When she looked up, Howdy was standing at her desk.

"You're out!" she said and immediately regretted it. It sounded like he'd been in prison. Howdy took no offense. In fact, he looked happy to see her and was professionally attired in a dark blue suit, white shirt, and striped tie. He smiled at her.

"I've been released, yes. I'm okay now. I've recovered from the shock of Alicia's passing. But I need your help, Emily. Will you help me?"

Emily thought his demeanor was both sane and sincere.

"Of course! What can I do?"

"You know the police still haven't found out who killed my fiancée?"

"Yes. I've called a few times myself for an update. It must be very frustrating and disheartening."

"Well, I'm tired of waiting for them. They told me that you found her body. I want to go back there and look for clues. I'm sure the police overlooked something."

"OK." She replied cautiously. "Did you want to go back there this weekend?"

"No, I want to go now."

"Now? But we have work to do."

"No, we don't. The computers are down, and I heard they'll be offline until at least noon. I don't think Rick's coming in today. Kathy has a training class. Nobody will even know we're missing."

"I don't know, Howdy; it seems pretty chancy."

"Come on. You owe me one. I covered for you the time…"

"Okay. You're lucky I can walk in these shoes and the sun's shining. We should be able to get there and back by ten. Do you have a coat?"

"No, I don't need one. Get your car keys and let's go."

Emily was feeling a little pissed. She carefully wrapped her muffin and stowed it in a drawer. She put the coffee in a back corner of her desk where it couldn't get spilled if an IT person came by to look at her PC. Then she pulled her purse from a desk drawer, and they walked through the still empty floor to the elevators.

When they got to her car, Howdy folded himself into the back seat so that he couldn't be seen from the outside. He removed his jacket and placed it over his head, and because of his slight stature, he was barely noticeable in the semidarkness of the garage.

"Why are you hiding in the back seat?" Emily asked.

"I'm not supposed to leave the building. Part of my conditional release from the Rockford Center. But, come on, we're adults. I'm okay. I really want to solve Alicia's murder."

Though a little uncomfortable with this scenario, Emily admired his determination and acquiesced to his plan.

As she was driving out of the building, the guard stopped her again.

"Why are you leaving so soon?" he asked, eyeing her with suspicion.

"I left something at home. I'm going back to pick it up," Emily lied. She didn't know what else to say.

"OK," he said and let her go.

Relieved, she drove up the short ramp toward the street. Rick's BMW was pulling in.

"Uh-oh, Here's Rick," Emily said. He slowed down and gave her a quizzical look. Howdy poked her in the ribs and growled, "Keep going. I don't want *him* on my case."

Emily did as he suggested.

As she pulled away, she looked at her rearview mirror and saw several policemen with guns drawn appear from the shadows of the building supports and surround Rick's car. What the hell was that about, she wondered. But Howdy was still poking her in the ribs to urge her on, and she was too flustered to think clearly.

It took them only fifteen minutes to drive out Pennsylvania Avenue to Route 100 and then onto Rockland Road and into Brandywine Creek State Park. There were no cars in the parking lot and no one on the paths. Emily guessed the time to be roughly eight o'clock or maybe a few minutes before. Perhaps the park office didn't open until eight thirty or nine on a weekday.

Howdy carefully followed behind her as she made her way up to the break in the wall where Alicia's body had been found. A chill wind had sprung up during their drive, and the dark gray clouds seen earlier in the day had grown ominous and begun to gather. Emily put her hands in her pockets and scrunched her shoulders together to keep warm. The cold didn't seem to bother Howdy.

"Here it is," Emily said, indicating the spot where police tape was still strung along dead tree branches and withered bushes. "What do you think we should be looking for?"

"I don't know, let's just get down on our hands and knees and comb through the grass."

"Get down on our hands and knees? Howdy, I'm all dressed up for work. And you have on a suit. I'm not getting down on my hands and knees. I can crouch down a little…" Emily did this as she was talking, and the next thing she knew, Howdy had pushed her onto the ground.

"We need to talk," he said. "I needed to get you alone."

"Alone?" Emily felt she was missing some crucial piece of information. Was this some bizarre romantic tryst?

"You know too much. You've been snooping into everyone's business. You know about the Owls, and you know about Alicia, and you've probably figured out that I killed her."

This was a confession—and bad news. Why would he confess to her? Perhaps he was delusional. Emily knew she was in deep trouble now. The park was deserted. No one could see them.

"You? No, Howdy, I didn't know you killed her. I actually thought maybe someone in the Owls did. Or maybe even Rick."

"Rick is the problem! Rick knows everything. He knows about the Owls, and he knows I killed Alicia, and he's using that to blackmail me into having sex with him."

This was a shocker! Emily stopped worrying about herself for a nanosecond and contemplated how it all fit together. She had seen Rick's exaggerated attention to Howdy and guessed that Howdy must have been suffering some sexual confusion of his own. But she didn't know what the connection was to the Owls.

"What is there to know about the Owls?"

"That they've hacked into the bank's computer system. They're destroying it right now with worms or viruses or whatever it is they use to delete files. They're wiping out everyone's mortgages and credit card bills so that no one who has accounts with Mirety Bank will have any debt. It's brilliant. But I was afraid that Alicia was going to tell Security."

"I thought you loved her. You were going to marry her, weren't you?"

"Once, maybe, I wanted to. But I changed my mind."

As Emily began to gather her wits, she realized she should keep him talking and try to calm him down.

"It's a big step. It's natural to have second thoughts. Did you talk to her about it?"

"I tried to, but she didn't understand. It's not just marriage, it's the bank...and Rick...and being responsible for making someone else happy."

"Yes, marriage is a lot of responsibility." Maybe agreeing with him would sidetrack him, she thought.

"*Everything* is too much responsibility. Work, love, sex, the world. I can't handle it all. *I just can't handle it all!*"

Howdy shouted this last sentence. Sweat was dripping from his forehead even in the chill air, his eyes were wide and crazed, and Emily began to feel very frightened. She tried another tactic.

"Well, it looks like you got away with it," she said, sounding upbeat and rational.

"Greg suspected. He would have told you eventually, and then you would have told the police."

"No, I wouldn't. Believe me, Howdy, I won't tell anyone."

"Yes, you will, and I have to make sure you don't."

He put his hands around her throat and pressed his thumbs into her windpipe. She hadn't thought he would actually harm her. Maybe just threaten her. She began to choke and tried to push him off her. They tumbled around on the wet grass. She kneed him clumsily in the groin, and he loosened his grip a tad but recovered quickly and squeezed tighter. She knew that strangulation took longer than it looks on TV, but panic was beginning to overwhelm her. With all the strength she could muster, she overcame her revulsion for what she was about to do. She took her thumbs, raised them to his face, and pressed them deeply into the inside corner of his eyes to gouge his eyes out. Howdy yowled in pain and let go of her.

Emily grabbed at this chance and took off at a run, not even sure of where she was going, hoping it was toward the park office. Her total focus was on getting away, not in pausing to figure out which was the best direction. She tried to lose him by heading down a muddy path that wound through low-hanging clumps of tree foliage and overgrown bushes. She couldn't hear him behind her, but she kept going anyway for what seemed like forever. Suddenly she found herself at the river.

Once there, she stopped to listen for Howdy following behind her, but heard nothing. She took a few breaths, then was startled by a crashing sound of arms and legs coming through the brush.

"Emily!" he shouted.

She didn't respond. She had to keep going.

She ran and continued running even as her legs began to ache and her lungs burn. She scrambled through the riverbank foliage that tugged at her skirt and tore holes in her panty hose. Her heart was pounding nearly out of her chest. She began to feel dizzy and nauseous. It seemed like she'd been running for at least a mile. The park office was not along the river, and she had no idea where a path was that would lead her to it. Her confusion about her bearings only added to her pain. When it began to rain, it was a blessing, its chill keeping her alert like a cold washcloth during a migraine.

She traveled maybe a quarter of a mile, but it was a quarter of a mile of misery. She wasn't sure if she could keep up this pace for very long, and she didn't know what was ahead. Either way, up or down the river, she should come to a road or a parking lot.

She momentarily took her eyes off the bushes to look up and through the dense clumps of leaves and twigs. She thought she caught a glimpse of blonde hair up ahead. Was someone there? She was afraid to yell as she didn't know how close behind Howdy was following.

The hope of stumbling onto someone who could help her gave her new strength. She pressed her feet down a little harder, trying to pick up momentum, and pushed more forcefully at the undergrowth blocking her path. She was assaulted with stings and scratches to her face and hands. Every muscle and bone in her body ached. She looked up again, and the blonde head appeared a little closer, but still turned away from her. "Please," she called as loud as she dared, "can you help me?" There was no response.

As she ran her thoughts were racing. Since the morning she'd found Alicia's body, she had been trying to figure out who had a motive to kill her. Now it occurred to her how wrong she had been. She hadn't needed to waste all that time looking at motive. It was so simple. All she had needed to ask was who took Alicia to the park that night. The answer was obvious—Howdy. What an idiot she had been!

She continued her charge through the briars and brambles for another forty or fifty yards, feeling sure she would pass out any second. Rain soaked her hair and clothes and dripped off her face. Every so often she would look up and see the blonde head always another ten or so yards ahead of her. She kept up her soft pleas for help, calling louder now as she felt sicker and sicker, but the head never turned around.

At last she came to the spot where Adams Dam Road crossed the Brandywine. Here she scrambled up the embankment and stood on the macadam, allowing herself to breathe a sigh of relief at last. There was no blonde-headed woman, however, waiting for her. When a red Camry came around the bend, she waved her arms and felt immense relief as it came to a stop.

"What happened to you?" asked an elderly man who opened the passenger door for her.

"You don't want to know," Emily said, smiling at him gratefully in between gulps of breath. "Can you take me to the office at Brandywine Creek State Park?"

"Of course. Here, have a Kleenex. Have you been hurt? You have dirt on your face."

"I was chased by someone," she explained. "I'll call the police when I get to the office."

Emily sat in the front seat and took deep breaths of air, looking out the windows for a glimpse of Howdy running through the bushes or walking on the road. There was no sign of him.

The stranger kindly deposited her at the office where Emily noted with relief that her car was still in the parking lot and there were more cars now parked near the office door. She went in and spoke to Denise, the receptionist, who looked at her with wide eyes and gaping mouth.

Before Denise said a word, Emily said "Please call 9-1-1. I was just assaulted in the park."

Emily sat on a wood bench as she waited for the police. Denise got her a cup of hot coffee and some wet paper towels for her scratches. She drank the coffee first to warm her, but as she sipped the strong brew, she was thinking of the blonde-haired person who had guided her through the woods to the road and then vanished. Who had it been? Then she heard a whisper in her ear, although she was sitting all alone in the park office while Denise ran to greet the police who had just arrived—lights flashing, sirens blaring. It was just a whisper, but Emily heard it as clearly as church bells or train whistles. "It's me, Alicia. Thank you."

CHAPTER THIRTY-TWO
BACK TO THAT FIRST SATURDAY NIGHT

The night air was uncommonly soft and warm for October. The breeze had died down. Even the crickets were silent, as if in awe of the light show playing out across the sky. Falling stars streaked across the heavens five and ten at a time, so fast and so numerous Alicia couldn't follow them all at once. There was a streak to her left, then to her right, then three or four gracefully plummeting through the blackness in front of her.

"Tell me about the Band of Owls, Howdy. How are they going to remake the world?"

"I don't want to talk about the Owls right now," he replied.

"But I thought that's why you wanted to see me tonight. Look, I got this tattoo. It's a symbol of my commitment."

They had been lying on their backs on a green wool blanket to watch the Draconids, but now Alicia turned over and pulled up the bottom of her white top to show Howdy the new tattoo of the owl on her back. He glanced at it briefly.

"In my mind, tonight is a mystical marriage of two portentous events," Alicia went on to say. "The falling stars in our universe and the collapsing financial system in our country. I want to be a part of it. I want to see Mirety Bank go under and all those mortgage and credit card loans lost in a black hole of computer dysfunction so that everyone is freed of their soul-crushing debt. When are they going to hack into the computers?"

"I'm not sure when. And I've been told to tell you that you can't be a part of that. The other Owl members don't trust you. They're afraid you'll tell someone at the bank about their plans. They don't want you at any more of their meetings."

"I got this tattoo for nothing." Alicia hung her head, her hopes of being part of a solution dashed to bits.

"I had another reason for meeting you tonight," Howdy continued. "I thought our enjoying the meteor shower would make it easier to tell you."

"Tell me what."

"I've decided I don't want to get married."

"What? I don't understand. I thought you loved me."

"I do. I do love you. But I've been thinking about my life and how I want to live it. Since I've been with the Owls, I can see the hypocrisy of modern society. How we're all just working for the almighty dollar. How we're all slaves to business and the government and the economy. I want a different life. I want to be free."

"What does that mean? You 'want to be free.' Nobody's really free. We all have things we have to do to survive."

"I don't want a conventional life. I hate my job at the bank. I hate pretending to be management material and all the bullshit that entails."

"That's okay. You can get a different job. We can still get married."

"You don't understand. I don't want marriage and children and a mortgage and all that bourgeois stuff. I don't want to have to work for a living."

"How can you not work for a living? What do you want to do?"

"I want to paint and listen to music and hang out with my friends. Some of us guys from the Owls are going to California. After a few months' residence, we can collect food stamps and get free medical care. Life is too short to spend it in an office." He didn't add that he was tired of Rick and his plans for him. Rick thought he was bisexual, but he wasn't. He had just been stringing Rick along for the free dinners and attention. He was disgusted with it now. He wanted to leave—his job, his girlfriend, his life.

Alicia sat up. All her dreams had just been blown away, like a tornado descending and sucking up all the houses and pulling up all the trees. She could hear the wind howling in her ears. Everything was gone. No great cause, no husband, no home, no children, no future—nothing. She looked around her with angry eyes and saw only a blighted landscape—no park, no sky, no tomorrow.

"How can you do this to me?" she hissed at him. She hardly knew what she was doing when she took her right fist and punched him square in the gut. It didn't seem to register on him. He just stared at her.

"What kind of man are you?" she railed at him. His only response was to take her right hand in both of his.

"A man who wants a new life, with new friends, and no responsibilities."

"You're not a man at all," she scoffed. "You're just a little boy." The pain of her loss, all her hopes and dreams dashed, this was a pain she needed to share—no, not just share, to inflict. The words were in her mouth, so cruel, she knew. She spat them out, "You little fairy."

Something in Howdy broke. Alicia never had the chance to speak again.

CHAPTER THIRTY-THREE

Hello and Good-Bye

Emily was relieved to see that it was Eastlake and Smith who had responded. She described what had happened, her voice low and steady as she blinked back tears, reliving the terror of the attack and her run through the park. Eastlake sat grim-faced during her recital of the events. Smith seemed a bit bored, as if he'd heard it all before. His call to pick up Howdy was cursory and perfunctory. After her brief statement, they let her go home to change and clean up.

As she was describing it all again to Melinda and Elvis, the phone rang. It was Eastlake calling to tell her they'd picked up Howdy hitchhiking on Route 100. She reassured Emily that she had nothing to fear as Howdy would be held without bail. One murder charge, one attempted murder, and one attempt at flight wouldn't sit kindly with the judge at the bail hearing.

"Will you be informing the bank of Howdy's arrest?" Emily asked.

"That's my next call. You should also know that Rick Wiseburg was arrested but has already been released on bail. He's not allowed to enter the bank or access any of its files either through the computer or by asking employees to provide him with hard copies."

"Why was Rick arrested?" Emily asked, surprised.

"We have evidence he knew about the planned attack on the computer systems. That's all I can tell you for now."

"Do you think he has any reason to come after me?"

"I don't know what it would be. You should be okay."

Emily did not feel reassured.

She returned to work after a quick cleanup and a bite of lunch. She surprised herself—and Melinda and Elvis—with her composure. She wondered at her own lack of reaction to the recent events. She knew women who would have been in tears and needed two or three days off from work to recover. She guessed she was made of stronger stuff.

At her desk, there was a phone message from Bob asking her to call him. She did so immediately.

He told her he'd heard what had happened. "Are you sure you're okay? Would you like me to call John Joseph and reschedule the interview for you?"

"Honestly, I'd rather be busy. Even though the computers are still down, I can always do filing until the interview." Emily was grateful for Bob's concern.

She had no sooner replaced the receiver in its cradle than it rang loudly. Picking it up, she was shocked to hear Rick's voice on the line.

"I need to speak to you right away," he said. "Can you come to O'Friel's? I'm in a booth in the back corner. Don't tell anyone where you're going."

"Are you sure this is okay? I know you're not allowed in the bank. Are you allowed to contact bank employees?"

"I'm your boss, Emily. And innocent until proven guilty. I just want to talk."

"Okay," she reluctantly agreed, unable to think of a reason to decline.

This time, as Emily made the transition from sidewalk sunshine to the bar's dark-paneled obscurity, there were no flowery shampoo scents of just-washed hair to remind her of a missing girl. There was just a feeling of apprehension churning in her stomach. Hadn't she been through enough today?

She found Rick at a far booth, a half-empty mug of beer on the table and a sour look on his face.

"Are the systems back up?" he asked?

"No," she answered, sliding into the seat opposite him.

"They would be if they'd let me take charge of the reboot." He started to fold and unfold his napkin in annoyance.

"Did their outage have anything to do with the police being here earlier?"

"Yes. Seems I was right about the bank's being the target of a terrorist group. Most of our data is gone, but they're working on retrieving it. I don't know yet how successful they'll be. I've been in conversations with the police, but for some reason, they suspect that I had a role in it, and I've been locked out. Just came back from the police station. I heard what happened to you. I know Howdy has been arrested. I underwent the third degree myself. Luckily, I'm pretty savvy about these things, and I have a crackerjack attorney. You look like you're okay. Are you?" He was still frowning.

"I will be." So much for his concern for her well-being.

"I hear you're jumping ship just when I've lost my other best employee," he said. "You really know how to hurt a guy."

"What are you talking about?"

"You have an interview with Global Loans, and I'm told you've got some dispensation from Human Resources to take this position before your year with me is up."

"I haven't got the job yet. I don't know how the interview is going to go. Maybe they won't offer me a job."

"Oh, they will. And now my best boy is arrested for murder. How screwed can one manager be?"

"I'm sorry if this is such an inconvenience for you," Emily said, trying to keep the sarcasm out of her voice. She was still inwardly laughing at his describing his arrest as "conversations with the police."

"You know, " she said sadly, "I had no idea about Howdy. It's horrible."

"Yes, it is." Rick turned pensive. "Guess my warning phone call to you about Bob didn't do any good. Don't come crawling to me asking for your old job back when things don't work out over there."

"That was *you*?"

"Have to protect my territory. Just remember to tell the higher-ups that I always treated you right. Give me a good report. Okay?"

"Sure." Like hell she would.

"I do have a favor to ask, though. I need some files that are sitting on top of the gray cabinet in the corner by the window. Do you think you could bring those to me? I'll be here for an hour or so."

"You know I can't do that, Rick. The police told me you're not allowed to access any of your files."

"Don't you think you owe me a favor or two for sticking by you when all the complaints came in about your lousy training?"

Complaints? The idea angered Emily. The only ones Emily knew of were what she'd overheard in the ladies' room. He was lying. Shaking her head, she said, "Sorry. I can't risk getting caught."

"Well, you'd better hope Global Loans picks you up, 'cause

you'll be history on my staff." He lifted his beer mug and took a sip, then set it down and looked away.

"I understand. I'd better go."

Emily got up and walked away, trembling just slightly at the bridge she'd just burned. *That job in Global Loans had better work out,* she thought. Wasn't it typical that Rick would make it all about him?

Emily got a call later from Detective Eastlake. Howdy had broken down and given the police the names of the Band of Owls' members who were responsible for the sabotage at Mirety Bank. They'd arrested Alicia's brother Greg, but when they discovered that he had sent the audiotape, they let him go. There was an APB out for Wyatt Dennison and a few other Owl members.

This was the first Emily had heard about Greg and an audiotape.

"Greg? Audiotape?" Emily was bewildered.

Eastlake explained, "One that Greg made at an Owls' meeting discussing details of the sabotage. I guess he saw it as a bargaining chip if he were caught. He has all the major players on tape, including your boss Rick Wiseburg."

"Rick?"

"Yes! Please be careful around him."

"Don't worry," Emily said with a shake of her head that the detective couldn't see but could hear in her voice. "I always give him a wide berth." She thought it best not to mention seeing Rick and his request. "What do you think will happen to him and the others?"

"Howdy has been charged with the murder of Alicia and kidnapping and assault upon you. The Owls and your boss will be charged for cyber-crimes, grand theft, and conspiracy. They'll all do jail time, I'm sure. Howdy may be facing life in prison."

"It's so unbelievably sad. I would never have suspected Howdy of being capable of such behavior."

"We'll be in touch," Eastlake said, ending the conversation.

"Thank you," Emily said and hung up the phone.

Feeling unsettled and at loose ends, she left her desk and went down to the cafeteria. With the computers still inoperable, there was little she could accomplish at her desk anyway. The cafeteria was closed, but coffee was still available. She treated herself to an extra-sugared and vanilla-flavored decaf, then took her cup to the lounge area and found a comfortable chair. She needed to absorb all that had happened to her. Not just the physical hurts—the cuts and bruises and sore muscles—but her moral outrage that was provoked by what she would call, for lack of any other word, the "evil" in the world.

She had escaped from Howdy, but his threat had been a straightforward physical one. The more dangerous threat was Rick. He represented an immoral universe that she could not combat. She was not a crusader. She was not an organizer. She had barely survived her divorce and the exploitation of the corporate workplace. She played by the old rules: work hard, treat others as you would want to be treated, and hope to be rewarded. But the truth was that people like her were not rewarded. They were used and patronized and overworked, while the raises and promotions went to someone else.

She comforted herself with the thought that she didn't want to be a part of a management group that was populated by men like Rick Wiseburg. She was a grunt, an ant, someone to be used up and spit out. And any glory she accumulated was in accepting her place and doing her job with grace and intelligence. The schemers and manipulators might beat her down, but she went home at night with a clear conscience. Not many of the suits in the corner offices could say that. She was so tired of it all.

Her better self rallied and suggested that she blame her sudden funk on her physical exhaustion. She straightened her shoulders and finished her coffee. Time to get back on the treadmill.

Emily arrived promptly at four for her interview in Global Loans. She was a bit taken aback by the manager, a man—or a boy, really, in contrast to her—of mixed European and Middle Eastern heritage, who greeted her warmly and introduced himself as John Joseph. He pointed out a chair for her to sit down in and immediately launched into a description of her job duties.

"I'll be training you myself," he explained. "I'll show you where client information is stored, how you'll receive loan requests, how to send the money out, and all the spreadsheets you'll need to complete monthly. Everything is done with email or fax, except for an occasional telephone call. Even those calls, though, you'll want to document with a follow-up email."

"How many accounts will I be responsible for?" Emily asked.

"About fifty or sixty. You have three coworkers who are handling all of them now. They'll be glad to see you."

"Is there overtime?" This was a tricky question and had to be asked in a manner that suggested she was not reluctant to put in the necessary hours to get the job done. She also didn't want to appear to be a poor money manager who required overtime to meet her household bills.

"Usually at quarter end when businesses need a quick cash injection to cover expenses and quarterly reports are due, but the rest of the time you should be able to leave at five."

"Have you done this job yourself?" she asked.

"Oh, yes. I did it for eighteen months before I was promoted. I created the manual you'll be using. If you have any problems, just ask me. What do you think? Are you interested?"

"Yes. I'd love to work in Global Loans." She meant it. To have a boss that understood her job and could be counted on to assist her when there was a problem, that was pure gold in the corporate world.

"Wonderful. You'll start the first of November. I'll notify Human Resources."

Back on her floor to check the computer system one last time before going home, Emily ran into Kathy and Nora walking the aisles and shaking their heads.

"What's happening? Systems not up yet?" Emily asked.

"No," Kathy replied. "Latest word is that a virus has erased credit card and mortgage records for the past one hundred and eighty days and damaged the corresponding backup file info. They've killed the virus, but they can't retrieve the backup files. Although, I'm sure they've got the best techies in the company working on it."

"What happens to all our customers?" Emily asked.

"So far, all activity is at a standstill," Norah explained. "Credit cards are frozen. There's already been an announcement on the news, and Mirety stock is tanking."

"Tech Support claims it can retrieve data before six months ago and restore any lost accounts," Kathy said. "But they won't be able to do anything about accounts created afterward unless they can fix the backup file info. We're asking people to mail in their information in good faith."

"Wow. Customer Service will be busy," Emily said with dismay. "They'll need to hire temps to cover the extra work while our profits go out the door." She thought it best to keep quiet for now about her own exit. She hoped this current crisis wouldn't delay it. The bank would be needing trainers. Maybe this would be an opportunity for senior customer service personnel to be promoted to training positions. She could make that suggestion.

"I can't believe Rick had anything to do with this virus business," Nora said, trying to inject a soothing note. "I didn't like him, but I never thought he would do anything criminal. He was always nice to me."

"Believe it," Kathy said.

"Suppose Rick doesn't come back," Emily ventured.

"Oh my, Auntie Vie gets the promotion he's been waiting for!" Kathy blurted out. She looked at Emily and Norah, eyes wide. Emily had never seen her so upset. "I don't know whether to laugh or cry," she continued. "He's useless. We are totally screwed."

Epilogue

Emily was relieved her transfer to Global Loans was not jeopardized by the disastrous results of the virus launched by the Owls. With just enough reserves and lots of IT talent, the bank survived, although stockholders had to settle for a ten cent on the dollar devaluation.

By late November, Emily had settled on her home and moved in. The next day she planted winter-blooming pansies in the front yard—purple, yellow, orange, and white. They reflected the joyful colors of her heart. More importantly, she was putting down roots. This was her house. No one could make her leave. She was home at last.

On the evening of the first Saturday in December, Emily placed four white ironstone dishes around her oak dining table, laid out four place settings of stainless steel flatware, and folded four dinner napkins at each place. Next, she set out the butter dish, and the salt and pepper shakers. She took four wine glasses from the cupboard, then set the Duraflame log alight in the fireplace. The hors d'oeuvres—shrimp, cocktail sauce, cheese, and a variety of crackers—were laid out on the coffee table along with cocktail napkins with funny sayings about wine, women, and song. Everything was ready for her dinner guests. She knew Melinda and Elvis would enjoy themselves. She was just a little nervous about Bob. Her chicken recipe was straight from the pages of *Better Homes and Gardens.* She hoped it would be delicious.

When she answered the first knock at the door, she found Melinda standing there, alone, with a bottle of wine in her hand.

"Elvis has a surprise for you," Melinda said as Emily stood back to let her enter. "He wanted me to tell you first that if you don't like it, he can take it back to his cousin."

"Okay," Emily replied, though a trifle apprehensive. What sort of gift could be so questionable? "I can't wait to see what it is," she said. "Tell him to come in."

Melinda waved her hand out the door, and Elvis emerged from the car with a cardboard box. He slowly made his way up the walk, and as he carefully stepped, Bob pulled up and jumped out his car, running up to peek at what was inside.

Melinda whispered, "Oh no, he'll give it away."

Elvis must have shushed him because Bob only looked up at Emily and Melinda in the doorway and grinned.

Once he and Bob were inside, Elvis immediately set the box on the floor, and there she was, a tiny pure-black fur ball, with gold eyes, a sweet face, and little kitten paws caught up in a pink knitted blanket.

"Oh, I love her. It is a her, I assume, from the pink blanket?"

"Yes," said Elvis. "Do you like her?"

Emily picked her up. The kitten sat quietly in her palm. Emily stroked her head with two fingers. The kitten purred.

"She needs a name," Melinda said."

"It's Zoe," Emily said. "I don't know why, but she just looks like a Zoe. Welcome home, little one."

"Thank you," she added, looking up at Melinda and Elvis.

"Well, it looks like she's staying," Elvis said. "I'll get the kitty litter and other supplies from the car."

"I'll help you," Bob offered, and the men left.

"For once, I know what *you're* thinking," Emily said to Melinda. "What?"

"Men may come and go, but a pet is to love forever."

"Exactly."

THE END

Questions for the Author

Is the character of Alicia based on Anne Marie Fahey?

No. Alicia and Anne Marie are very different people. While they were both young and beautiful girls who were murdered, they had very different backgrounds, lifestyles, and boyfriends. Anne Marie had a large family who cared deeply about her, while Alicia had only her brother. Anne Marie had a prominent position as the governor's scheduling secretary, enjoyed beautiful clothes and fine dining, and looked forward to an upscale future with her fiancée. Alicia was in a low-paying, entry-level position with the bank and struggled to get by, pinning her hopes for the future on another lower-echelon bank employee. Anne Marie dated two handsome, successful men. Alicia only had Howdy. I can't picture Anne Marie joining a revolutionary type organization or acquiring a large tattoo.

Is there a real person on whom Alicia is based?

In the1970s, a young woman was killed in Brandywine Creek State Park. My memory of it is sketchy as it happened so long ago, and I was not able to find any details about her online. I believe she was shot. I never heard that the person who killed her was caught, but in doing research for this book, I was able to access a list of cold cases in Delaware and her murder was not among them. Therefore, I can only assume the perpetrator was found.

Unfortunately, I don't know anyone in law enforcement, and after asking all my friends and family, no one else recalls this case. I guess I was the only one who was touched by this story. I am hoping that none of the details have any resemblance to the real-life crime as I would not want to dredge up any painful memories for the family.

Are any of the male characters based on Tom Capano?
No, they are not. None of my fictional characters are ever based entirely on a real person. When I am creating a character, I borrow personality traits from a few people I know or have read about, mix them together, and then add a generous dollop of my own imagination. If you know me well, you may occasionally recognize a person, or pet, I've loved and lost.

Whose ghost was it in O'Friel's—Alicia's or Anne Marie's?
Your guess is as good as mine.

I want to thank all my readers
For accompanying me on this
Journey along the Brandywine.

Love and Peace to you all,
Maryellen Winkler

Follow the clues with Emily Menotti as she unravels still more mysteries:

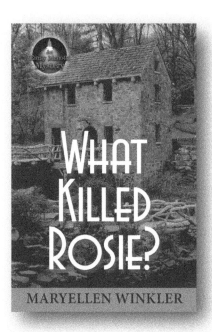

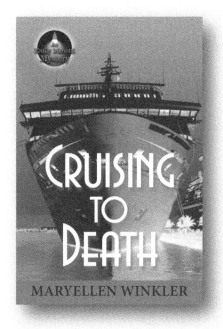

Who did Emily see in the laundromat doorway that warm May evening?

It looked like her old friend Rosie. Problem is, Rosie died of a heart attack five years ago, and now Rosie's old boyfriend is reporting strange occurrences at his condo. Is it Rosie's ghost demanding revenge? Or is someone trying to perpetuate a hoax? Join Emily as she searches among Rosie's acquaintances to find out what really killed Rosie.

Intrepid amateur sleuth, Emily Menotti, is on her first Caribbean cruise along with the Wayward Sisters book club. As they head out of New York City, however, a friend goes missing.

With the help of her clairsentient pal, Melinda, Emily starts investigating. Yet even a séance, guided by Melinda, reveals more old secrets than new clues.

Set amid tropical backdrops, this mystery has motives aplenty, including an ex-husband, a former high school boyfriend, and the ongoing resentment of two unmarried friends.

Join Emily as she solves the mystery on a chilling cruise with some uninvited passengers: jealousy, revenge, and death.

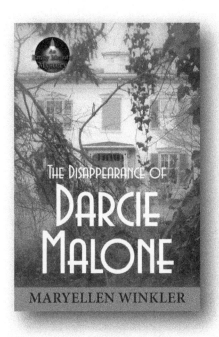

THE DISAPPEARANCE OF

DARCIE MALONE

MARYELLEN WINKLER

On a warm September night in 1969, a young couple embarks on a romantic midnight picnic on the grounds of a legendary haunted house. By morning, the girl has disappeared, and her boyfriend is found mentally confused and unable to speak. She is never found, and the mystery is never resolved.

Thirty years later, Emily stands in the dark and hears an old man singing, calling out for "Darcie." She turns to see who is singing, but no one's there.

Join Emily as she is drawn deeper into discovering what happened to Darcie Malone.

Emily Menotti Mysteries are available on Amazon.com.

CPSIA information can be obtained
at www.ICGtesting.com
Printed in the USA
JSHW021853051219
2735JS00002BA/15

9 781935 751489